• • • IN DUE TIME • • •

3.5.2

Thank You for
Supporting In Due Time.

Enjoy the book.

Nigel Keynum

• • • • IN DUE TIME • • • •

A Novel
By
NIGEL REYNARD

XandraFish Publishing,
Atlanta, GA

XandraFish Publishing
2221 Peachtree Road, Suite D-638, Atlanta, GA 30309

First Printing, February, 2002
06 05   04 03 02 01
Copyright © Nigel Reynard, 2002
All rights reserved

 TRADEMARK OF XANDRAFISH PUBLISHING

LIBRARY OF CONGRESS CATALOGING-IN-PUBLICATION DATA
Reynard, Nigel
In Due Time / Nigel Reynard
p. cm.
ISBN 0-9718393-0-1
1. Relationships—Fiction 2. African-American—Fiction
   3. Atlanta (Georgia)—Fiction 4. Clark Atlanta University—Fiction
   5. Los Angeles (California)—Fiction 6. Consulting—Fiction
   7. Newport News (Virginia)—Fiction 8. Weddings—Fiction
   9. Race Relations—Fiction 10. Labor Relations—Fiction
   11. Medical (Residency)—Fiction.
   I. Title.

813'.54—dc21   2002102413
Printed in the United States of America
Set in Garamond
Designed by Carol Addyman and Addyman Design

PUBLISHER'S NOTE
    This book is a work of fiction. Names, characters, places, and
incidents either are the product of the author's imagination or are used
fictitiously, any resemblance to actual persons, living or dead, events, or
locales is entirely coincidental.

This book is printed on acid-free Paper

Direct Inquiries to author at
nigel_reynard@hotmail.com or visit NigelReynard.com

Dedicated to

Louise B. Chandler-Wilson

Alice B. Armstrong

Chris Belle

We miss you

LIFE IS BUT A DREAM

1 . . .

I awoke in a cold sweat. It was 2 a.m. and I hadn't finished my report for my 9 o'clock meeting. I jumped up, took a shower and geared myself for being up the rest of the morning. Luckily I was prepared. I'd brought my laptop with me to Sandy's apartment. I don't know why. I just did. I guess it was a little bit of wishful thinking and a little bit of self-confidence that I would be spending the night. I kept saying I was going to stop letting Sandy be a disruption to my life. She was like a New Year's resolution that I resolute every three to four months.

I pulled the research from my computer bag. Oh Damn! I had forgotten the bottle of Mountain Dew I'd left in the freezer. I was glad it didn't freeze. I had to have my Mountain Dew for the caffeine. It was summertime. I can't stand coffee. I have often wondered to myself how people consume cups and cups of coffee between May and September. But they do. It is what it is.

I sat down and started to crunch the figures that hadn't balanced since yesterday afternoon. I thought having a small dinner and looking at something pretty while I ate would restore some clarity in what I had been missing from work. Let's just say a couple of hugs and kisses later, I was stumbling to the shower drowsy and in a panic that the man was going to be on my ass first thing in the morning.

I sat back at Sandy's desk and looked at her. She was lying in her bed. Damn...she was beautiful to me. Her complexion was a copper toned yellow with wavy sandy brown hair. She says that's how she got her name. Her elementary school friends labeled it for her and it stuck. Her real name is Lyndsey. Lyndsey Raquel Franklin. I looked over at the family picture she had on her desk. It was a picture of her, her mother and her father. I could see where she'd gotten all of her features. Her big eyes came from her father. But the copper flakes in her green eyes were undoubtedly her mom's.

Sandy's mother, Antoinette was a high maintenance Creole sister who was biracial herself. She went to Chicago during the sixties escaping from an identity crisis she was experiencing in segregated Baton Rouge, Louisiana. Sandy told me that her mom went to Chicago because growing up she was a 'Nigga' to white folks and a 'Honkey' to black folks.

I could see why brothers would think she was white. I was looking at the picture and could only see specs of African-American myself. Maybe in her lips and a little in her nose. Her father was dark, a chocolate brother. What we would call a blue-black field nigger. He had played football at Central State in Ohio.

But Huey Franklin didn't act like a field nigger. In fact, more like a smart nigger. He was one of Chicago's top attorneys. Her mom was a schoolteacher at the Horace Mann School on the south side of Chicago. The two met at one of the school's Annual Leadership Day Programs. Her dad was the guest speaker. I joked with Sandy that he thought he was making a little money and the only thing missing was a "pink toe." He thought he had one, but he kept her mom anyway after he found out she was actually a sister.

Sandy was sleeping peacefully as she rolled onto her left side. She was sleeping like a baby who had gotten her last pacifier for the evening. She'd positioned the blue satin sheets between her legs while her right arm rested under her head. She mumbled something and rolled over. Yellow ass was everywhere. I wondered to myself why her bottom is the same color she is. Her whole body was one tone. I looked at my bottom and wondered why my chest and thighs were a light brown and my ass was like a Hershey's special chocolate. She has the most perfect body. Some of it was natural genetics, the other a track and field physique. She ran at Northwestern for four years. You could see the natural six-pack formed in her stomach. I had worked on my abs for the last three years to get them where I wanted them.

I met Sandy at the Chevron service station at Cascade and I-285. We were both getting gas. I was coming from a movie with an old girlfriend. She was coming from a house party in the Cascades, a wealthy subdivision on the Southside of downtown Atlanta. What the northsiders called "the black side." We just called it the SWAT, Southwest Atlanta.

Sandy's first words were, "Can I have that shirt?" She was pointing to the shirt I was wearing.

I replied, "Yeah. Are you coming to my house to get it?"

"No, I want you to take it off right here and give it to me."

I laughed, "Do I have sucker written across my forehead?" She laughed too.

"Where are you coming from?"

I stumbled across my words finally saying that I had been to a movie.

"With who?" She didn't hesitate to ask. I liked her spunk.

"By myself."

"Why we got to start this relationship off with a lie?"

"I ain't lying." I was lying my ass off. Ten minutes ago I was begging my ex-girlfriend for some ass. She had promptly denied me and sent me home with a kiss on the cheek and a thank-you for the movie. Evidently I had been a bad liar, Sandy's girlfriend who was sitting on the passenger side of her convertible 240SX was laughing as well.

I asked, "Why are ya'll laughing at me?"

Sandy replied, "Cause we know a brother as fine as you are, did not go to the movie by himself."

I lied again, "But I did."

"Whatever brotha, here's my number. Maybe we can go out for a drink after work sometime."

My body language must have concurred because I instantly began searching for a pen to give her my number too. I gave her the number. We said our good-byes. I backed into the doorway of my car focused on the devilishness of her smile and thinking to myself.

"You are a beautiful sista."

As she began to drive away, she asked me laughing, "Aren't you going to pump your gas? You already paid for it, right?"

"Damn!" I hadn't pumped an ounce of gas. And that's how Sandy and I hooked up.

It was now 5 o'clock in the a.m. and I was concentrating hard on the numbers for my report. At that moment, Sandy jumped straight up from her sleep. She startled me. She had had a nightmare. That wasn't like Sandy. She was usually a sound sleeper.

"Baby, what's wrong?"

"I had a bad dream."

"What was it about?"

She ignored my question, got out of the bed, and headed for the kitchen. Her butt-naked body moved so gracefully. Her walk was even sexy. Something inside tells me she'll be my wife someday. She opened the refrigerator and grabbed the carton of Minute Maid Citrus Punch. She turned up the carton like a gangsta turning up a forty of Olde English

Malt Liquor.

"Why are you even up this early?" She asked still dazed.

Sandy walked out of her way picking up the hairpin sitting on the edge of the desk. She stopped to see what was on the screen of my laptop. An intentional move, I had already deducted. As she passed, she leaned over the back of the chair and started to kiss the back of my neck. I lost a little of my concentration as the goose bumps rose like my mother's biscuits on a Saturday morning.

"Come back to bed. I need you." She insisted. "Kiss me."

She swung the chair away from the laptop and straddled my thighs. Putting herself between the screen and me.

"I can't play now. I've got to finish this stuff. Having this done before 9 pays my bills. I like to eat. It's essential to my livelihood."

She looked away. I sensed her irritation.

I asked my original question again, "What happened? What was the dream about?"

"Dream?"

"The dream, Sandy."

She hesitated, "You, me, and Kevin were in the bed together."

Suddenly, it hit me like a ton of bricks. I fell back into my space in this relationship. I was the other man.

2 . . .

I arrived at work about 8:15. I planned on getting there about 7, but sleep deprivation and dealing with Sandy had put me behind schedule. My boy Mike rolled up to my cubicle about 8:25, saying that Johnson was on his period. He lost seventy thousand dollars in the stock market yesterday. He had bragged a year ago that eighty percent of his stock was held in tech stocks and advising everybody to follow his lead. Today, he was hitting rock bottom in a hard way and any of us would too, if we did anything to piss him off.

I told Mike thanks for the warning. He pressed on to warn the rest of our clique about Johnson.

I printed my report. Proofed it and rolled into my 9 a.m. meeting. For the most part, I came from the meeting unscathed minus a few 'get your heads out of your asses' which were directed at all of us.

I got back to my cubicle around 11:30. Mike was back. He said he felt like he had been through combat. He joked that the meeting was like dodging land mines. I really wasn't hungry, but he pressed me for a lunch date with the fellas. I finally agreed telling him I could clear some of my workload by noon. He said cool, he would meet me at the receptionist's desk.

The phone rang. Who was it now? I checked the caller-

ID. It was Geena.

"Hello."

"Where were you last night?"

"I got caught up with some reports."

"The ones that were giving you trouble at work yesterday?"

"Hell yes."

"Goodness, did you finish?"

"Finally."

"We need to celebrate. Let some stress off. Boney James is going to be at the Sky Bar in Buckhead tonight. I got tickets. You want to go?"

"Cool. I'm game."

I'll meet you at your house at 7.

"It's a date. See you at 7. Look beautiful." I threw in a request.

"Always. Do you want me to bring the Eric Jerome Dickey book you left it over my house."

"No. Don't worry about it. I'll get it another time."

We hung up. I ran to the front to meet Mike, Rich, and Dave.

We decided to go to Mumbo Jumbo's on Park Place. It was a nice spot to entertain clients. In fact, last week I saw Brian McKnight sing a song for a brother who was proposing to his girl. It was off the chain.

At lunch, all we could talk and laugh about was Johnson and how much money he lost in the market.

Mike said, "I bet he'll move that shit now."

Dave said he was talking to his broker when we left for lunch.

Rich was cool as hell. He didn't care about shit. Whether the market rose or fell. Whether he got paid or didn't. He was the coolest white boy I had ever seen. We would ride to lunch with Rich sometimes. It was nothing for him to have Notorious B.I.G. in the disc changer. Dave would tell him to cut that shit off. But Mike would

intervene and start rapping just to irritate Dave and make
him feel like the odd man out. Dave would say tomorrow
he was rolling out his rickety '87 Accord, so he could play
his Smash Mouth or Sugar Ray CD's. We all liked those
groups too so it would just piss Dave off even more. But it
was all in good fun. We were Smith and Boland's four
musketeers, two brothers and two white guys. But I figured
Rich didn't care for two reasons. One, because he was 28
years old and still lived with him parents. ...And two,
because they were rich as hell and lived off West Paces Ferry,
a few blocks from the governor's mansion.

On several occasions Rich had asked me to set him up
with some sisters, which I refused telling him a little Pac
and Biggie was not going to prepare him for that thang a
sister was going to put on him. After several months of
begging, I decided to set Rich up with Deidre, a harmless
sister from undergrad at Clark. I set him up with Deidre
because I always thought that if anybody would flow to the
other side, it would be her.

A couple of days later, Rich came by cubicle to say
thanks for the hook up.

He surprised me when he said, "Bro, the sex was good."
I was surprised and kinda jealous because I had been after
her cute ass since freshman year.

We got back to work about 1. We came back on time
today. Nobody was fucking with Johnson. Might even
throw in some unsolicited overtime for general principle or
as we say GP. After putting in the grind for 4 more hours,
I was spent and decided not to work late. I had almost
forgotten that I was meeting Geena at my apartment in two
hours. I rushed out of the building and ran to the Five
Points MARTA Station to catch my train. It was always a
slow stroll because I liked to admire how beautiful Atlanta's
women are. But not today, I hurried past the fruit and fake
purse vendors who were hustling to make sales from the
evening rush. I barely caught the train. It was overfull, as

we say in the hood. But I squeezed in and mustied my way under a couple of 5 o'clock armpits to avoid a closing subway door. After about 3 stops, I was relieved and praising Jesus that he had answered my prayers for fresh air.

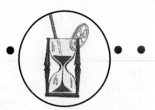

3 ...

My *doorbell* *rang* *about* *6:50*. It was Geena. I was still brushing my teeth. We've always had a complete role reversal when it comes to punctuality. She's always under the time and I'm always over it. I opened the door.

"What took you so long? Should have known you weren't ready."

I gargled out, "What are you talking about? I left work on time." She was talking as though I had control over public transportation.

"Yeah. Yeah. Yeah. As usual. But I love you anyway. Hurry up." Geena said as if she were in rush mode, but still grabbing the remote control to catch the latest news on Entertainment Tonight. The Puffy and J-Lo thing was big right now and everybody had an opinion.

I finished up and we headed to Buckhead. We decided to take her car because she was wearing a dress. But she wanted me to drive. It was cool. I didn't have a problem driving a 5 series BMW. It gave me an opportunity to get away from driving my Expedition. We decided to stop at the South City Kitchen for our before-concert dinner. They had an incredible banana cheesecake, which we always split when we ate there. We talked about what was going on in her life. What was happening in mine. I left a few things out. I wasn't really into discussing Sandy, with Geena anyway. After dinner, I stopped at the Martini Club next door and picked up some Felipe Gregorio premium cigars.

We got to the club about 9. Some local bands were opening for Boney. The vibe was cool. It was a nice mixed crowd. Black folks, white folks, as well as some Latinos and Asians. I am always impressed when I think back to 35 years ago and how this was a segregated city. Now there are very few places that are segregated. There was definitely a feeling that Atlanta was truly becoming the international city that it has always wanted to be, but fell short because of its racial divide. And now, we like their stuff and they like ours. Well, we aren't feeling the country music thing just yet. But I guess I'll put a check in all the other boxes.

Geena pointed out that there were even a few brothers with gold teeth representing at the Sky Bar tonight. I told Geena that thugs wanted their jazz too. We both laughed. I've always had a knack for making Geena laugh. She was looking especially good tonight. Her strapless blue dress laid on her body perfectly. Her neck and shoulders flaunted her caramel brown skin. I'd struggle to describe her as cocoa even though some people would. Her legs are the bomb. They're her best asset. Her legs made the Via Spiga shoes she wore look good. She's a cute girl. Not as gorgeous as Sandy, but would hold her own with any of the 7's or 8's strolling around Atlanta.

Boney was doing his thing. The crowd was definitely vibing. The brother standing next to me with his white girl said Boney was the whitest brother he had ever seen. Without saying a word, using only eye contact, Geena and I wondered if he was joking or if he was serious. I told Geena I hoped he was referring to Boney in the way we called Jason Williams of the Memphis Grizzlies, "White Chocolate."

Feeling the rhythm of the music, Geena backed her way into my chest and she wrapped my arms around her. Her hips swayed every other time the drummer hit a beat. I looked around because this venue was usually not where Geena and I vibed. It appeared to be cool. Fuck it, I just went with it. You only live once. Boney started to play I Will Always Love You. That was my song. I started singing in Geena's ear. She loved that. I always flirted with her in public. We had to stay like that for a minute, the smooth jazz and Geena's phat ass against my crotch had caused my nature to rise. I was a little embarrassed. I felt like I was back in 5th grade, 'peewee' was at attention, and my teacher was calling me to the blackboard. "No thank you Ms. Dean. I'd rather not answer that one." Geena assuredly felt me pressing against her derriere and acknowledged that it was okay. She didn't mind savoring the moment at my expense.

I looked to my right and saw this big brother and his girlfriend forcing their way to the front of the crowd. I was a little peeved by his rudeness and was prepared to tell him off if he crossed me. As they got closer, the girl started to become more recognizable even through the 3 Long Island Ice Teas I'd had. It was Sandy! The big brother must have been Kevin. They were drunk and laughing. Just having a good 'ol time. I was still holding Geena, just not as tightly. I wondered if he knew I was fucking his girl last night. Did he know she was calling my name and loving every inch of manhood I gave her? I was pissed. A little jealous, but it was neither the place nor the time to air dirty laundry.

As they moved through the crowd, Sandy and I made eye contact. She stopped for a second. The big guy must've thought that he lost her, so he looked behind him and pulled her forward.

When we went out, Sandy always looked very pop and girl next door. I'd never seen her the way she looked tonight. Her wavy hair was in cornrows that went along with the Baby Phat Jeans and her exposed midriff. I was dumbfounded by the B-girl look. Was that what he preferred? My girl was with another dude and not only that, she was 'straight thugging.' I wanted to call her mama and

daddy and ask them, "Do you know how Dr. Franklin is
dressed tonight?" But for right now I had to keep my
comments to myself.

Geena noticed my attention wasn't on Boney, but on the
girl across the room that looked our way from time to time.

"Who's she?"

"She who?" I looked everywhere but Sandy's direction.

"The light-skinned chick that keeps looking at us."

"How do you know she's looking at us?"

"A woman knows when another woman is looking at
her."

"Oh her... she dated Kareem for a minute."

"I didn't know Kareem had such good taste."

"He doesn't. That's why they ain't dating anymore."

Lyndsey Franklin's nosiness had gotten the best of her.
She gestured for us to come over where she and her date
were. I shook my head 'no'. But Geena wanted to go. She's
intrigued with meeting new people. She said, "Come on.
Let's go over there." I reluctantly agreed, but I knew some
shit was about to go down. There was a part of me that
wanted to stand face to face with the man who was sporting
my future wife. When we arrived, Geena said, "How are
you?"

I said to myself, "Why are you speaking? I haven't even
introduced you yet."

"I'm good. How are you? I'm Sandy."

"I'm Geena, the girlfriend."

"The girlfriend," Sandy repeated as she smiled and
giving me an evil eye that no one else in the world could
read but me. "This is a nice guy you have. Hold on to him.
He needs a good woman." As loud as the music was in the
club, I felt like I could have heard a pin drop when Geena
said she was the girlfriend.

"Well he's going to the curb if I don't get a ring for
Christmas."

"What?!!! You better get this girl a ring for Christmas."

Geena smiled in agreement, but I heard Sandy's sarcasm. There were 400 people in the club and the only two people who knew drama was going on, Sandy and me. The brother leaned over and introduced himself. I peeped his arm and saw we were fraternity brothers. I called him out. He gave me a bruh hug. I returned the endearment.

Sandy wasn't finished with the drama. She asked me, "So are you going to marry this woman or what?" Geena was good at instigating shit and laughing in the background.

"We've been dating for 8 years."

When she said that I could have melted through the floor. Kevin said, "Come on boss. Let's get some drinks. You ladies want anything?" Geena asked for a vodka and cranberry, while Sandy ordered her usual Cosmopolitan.

Geena acknowledged a bond, "So you're a vodka girl too."

"You know it."

Kevin said, "We got it. Let's hit the bar."

Kevin put his arm on my shoulder and escorted me to the bar. A part of me was scared to leave, I needed to stay and monitor the conversation. Another part of me wanted to smash my frat brother in the face. He was going out with my wifey.

I justified it thinking, "Hell, he ain't one of my sands."

Kevin talked all the way to the bar.

"So how do you know Sandy?"

Damn!!!...This brother asks too many questions.

"Dr. Franklin?"

"Oh, you were a patient?"

"Not really. We're just old friends. We met at First Friday a couple of years ago."

"She's a good girl."

"Are you asking me or telling me?" I quipped.

"I was telling you, dog."

"She is good people." I finally concurred.

Kevin ordered the drinks. I continued to investigate

Geena and Sandy's behavior. Their body language would tell
the story. I took a mental inventory of the exits just in case
I needed one. I tuned out everything in the room to see if
I could hear any parts of their conversation. Kevin was still
talking. It was like he was talking German. I thought to
myself, "Brother, what the fuck are you talking about? Can't
you see I got issues across the room?" Kevin said, "I'm
trying to get her to see my point. You feeling me?" I came
back to Kevin's conversation.

"You're right bruh." I didn't know what the hell I was
agreeing to. I sure hoped it wasn't about him marrying
Sandy.

"You need to tell her that shit. Y'all are friends."

"I will."

"Thanks bruh."

"How much do I owe you for the drinks?"

"It's on me dog."

" 'preciate it."

We walked back to the girls.

After being in a hurry to get back over to them, a part of
me wanted to hit an exit stage left. But I was a big boy. I
could handle the ass whipping I was about to get. I wasn't
afraid of Sandy, just jealous. I was afraid of Geena. She
could whip my ass, Xena style.

After a few dips and excuse me's, we arrived back. Sandy
said, "You have an interesting girlfriend." She was doing
that shit to fuck with me. Geena said, "I like her. We'll have
to invite Sandy to dinner." My mind was consumed. Why
were they playing these mind games? Just let me have it.
Put me out of my misery.

"Well Kev, let's get out of here. It was a pleasure
meeting you, Geena."

Sandy gave me one of her infamous big eye looks letting
me know we'll talk later. I saw it. No one else caught it, at
least not Geena. She hit me with one last jab before she left,
"You need to marry this girl. She's perfect for you." I

cringed to hear that from the woman I wanted to spend the rest of my life with.   Sandy and Kevin departed our presence.

"She's nice."

"She's cool. What did you guys talk about?"

"Did I ask you what you and your frat talked about?"

"No."

"Well then. Leave girl talk to the girls."

Lord, why was I being punished like this? Did I deserve this torture? Boney finished up his encore and we headed home. The ride home was quiet, at least on my part. Geena was rattling on about the concert and how Sandy was such a great person. She asked me why I hadn't introduced them sooner. I told her I didn't know. She said she gave Sandy one of her business cards. I had been discarding much of Geena's conversation, but that shit went through.

"Why would she need your business card?"

"She could be my step to a higher level of clientele."

"Why, are you tired of the Shanikas and LaWandas?"

"Ouch. Is something bothering you?"

"No. It has just been a long day."

"Well, when we get home I got something that will be put you straight to sleep." She giggled.

"Really?" I smiled back.

"I need a stress relief myself."

We arrived at my house. I took a shower. My mind was moving a million miles an hour. I put my drawers on underneath my PJ bottoms and got into the bed. Geena snuggled up underneath me. I pretended to start snoring. I could feel Geena's energy as she turned over and cursed me. Ten minutes later she was having a deep conversation with the sleep fairy. I got back up. Made some cocoa and sat on the patio. My thoughts were consumed by the events of the night. Kevin looked familiar to me. But from where? Was he a consultant? Undergrad? I couldn't put my finger on it. I jogged the hell out of my memory but he was just

untraceable. After about an hour, I gave up and took my ass
to bed.

4 . . .

I first met Geena in the 11th grade. We went to
Mays High School. Mays was the self-proclaimed
inner-city high school of the bourgeoisie, a school that was
one hundred percent black. It served to educate the kids of
ministers, civil rights leaders, doctors, lawyers, and a
handful of working class people that fell within district
lines.

Geena lived in London Townhouses not far from the
high school. Her mom was one of those working class
people. She drove a school bus for the city of Atlanta. She
moved the family from the East Lake Meadow Projects to
the Mays' school district so her kids could get a better
education.

I met Geena in Mr. Harrell's math class. She was smart,
fiery, and little street. When we first met she called me
"Preppy", because of my flat top fade and khaki pants. I
tried to fight it, but there was an undeniable attraction to
the girl from across the tracks. She was cool.

Geena had two brothers. One older. One younger.
Geena's older brother, Derrick graduated and went into the
Navy. He rarely returned home. He came home for
Christmas every two years, probably just to say he had a
family.

Her younger brother, Roland, was in prison.   He was
caught selling drugs in school.   Geena believed that he was
influenced by some new gangstas in the neighborhood that
had relocated from South Central Los Angeles.   She said she
spent time at my house because it gave her a sense of family.
Geena graduated fifth in our high school class.   I was
one hundred and fifth.   She chose not to go to college.   She
said her family couldn't afford the financial strain.   She went
to Atlanta Area Tech where she studied cosmetology.   She
wanted to do something where she could be making some
real money in less than two years.   Just like any other major
urban city, we had two salons on every block.   Having your
hair together in Atlanta was a must. A good haircut could
make or break a reputation and that's what Geena was
banking on.
She was out of AAT in eighteen months, burning wigs
and making money.   She enjoyed the fact that she was
independent.   She would sing Salt-n-Pepa's "Independent"
constantly.   She Cabbage Patched that song to death.   By
that time, we were inseparable.   She would come hang out
with me on weekends at CAU.
I ran short of funds once or twice.   She helped pay my
tuition sophomore and senior years.   I was greatful and
thankful for her. Her loyalty was above reproach.
When I was pledging, my sands and I hid at Geena's
house several weekends.   It was the one spot the Big
Brothers wouldn't find us.   We studied, talked, and relaxed.
It was like a weekend getaway.   Geena welcomed us with
open arms.   It was as if she was living the black college
experience vicariously through me.   I wouldn't do a thing to
change that.   She told me she needed it.   It was something
she missed out on.   I obliged her.
I sat and stared at her sometimes for hours.   It seemed
like just yesterday she was a mouthy adolescent.   I had
watched the mouthy adolescent blossom into a fine ass
woman and she was mine.   Well sometimes.   She hadn't

grown very much, though she had gone from eighty-five pounds to a one-twenty pound mature woman. We had broken up two, three, four times, only to get back together. Like Anita Baker's song "365 days", we used to break up to make up. She said I was her spirit. I didn't know about me being her spirit, but there was something permanent about the relationship.

When Geena felt my education exceeding hers, she soaked herself in my textbooks. You have to respect a self-taught sister. Hell, I came home one day and she was reading The Old Man and the Sea by Ernest Hemmingway. I had never read that shit. It was her way of saying, "Don't get ahead of me. You're not that smart. I was at the top of the class. Not you."

A couple of years ago, Geena got fed up with her bossy shop manager and quit. Within weeks she had opened her own salon off Campbellton Road and it was thriving. After all, she did have 45% of the clientele at the old salon. Geena was just a people person. You could take her to a barbeque or you could take her to a formal.

It wasn't until a couple of years later, when I met another girl at a gas station that I would begin to question our place in the cosmos.

5 . . .

$\mathcal{J}$ stumbled *out of bed and readied myself for work.*
Two late nights in a row, I was getting too old for this. Geena was still sleep. She didn't have to be at work until 11. Seeing her sleeping in made me wish I had pursued my own entrepreneurial dreams. But there was no time to think now. I had a 7:38 train to catch. I was out the door in 10 minutes.

I checked my voice mail when I got to work. I wanted to know if Sandy called. She didn't. Good. Maybe I'd never see her again. Never talk to her again. Never smell her again. She wasn't good for my psyche. She wasn't good for my ego. Hell, I'm a grown ass man and didn't need any girls playing games with me. I checked the voicemail again to see if I missed her call by accident. No Sandy. Good. I didn't want to talk to her anyway.

The phone rang about 9:30, it was Vlad, my boy from high school. Vlad was short for Vladimir. I often wondered why an African-American mother and father would give their son a Russian name. But it was cut off in school and we just called him "V".

"What's up, dog?"

"What's up, black?"

"Where've you been?" V questioned.

"Man, work has been kicking my ass."

"I can tell. You have been out of the flow. What's up with that?"

"I'm gonna make some time this weekend. Y'all shooting ball this weekend?"

"Saturday, 10 a.m. at Run 'n Shoot."

"Religiously. I should have known."

"You know. Come on down so I can put this schooling on you."

"Yeah right, then you woke up."

"Well come get some dog."

"I will. How's Marti?"

"You know, Marti's Marti."

"Tell her fine ass I said what's up."

"Hey! Hey! Hey! Don't be looking at my girl."

"Get worried if I stop looking. Let me get back to work. I got shit to take care of."

"I feel you dog. Do your thang. I'll see you Saturday."

"Take care bruh."

"You know."

We hung up.

V was my boy. I loved this guy like a brother. Once my car broke down 300 miles outside of Atlanta and he called in sick from work to come get me. That's a friend. We started at Clark together, but within two years he had gotten a job at the Ford Assembly Plant in Hapeville. He quit school altogether and never went back.

Here it was 12 years later. Me with a degree, he without one and he was making ten thousand dollars more than I was. Hell, he could have that shit. I didn't want to work in a body shop twenty years anyway.

V never had a problem with getting women. A thirty-year-old brother making $75,000 a year in Atlanta wouldn't have a problem meeting women anyway. He brought his women to his $200,000 bachelor pad in Fayetteville. He wined them, then dined them and made them think all that was his could be theirs too. That was his ploy to soak them in, get the panties and move on. But that was V.

He and Marti had been dating for five years. In the five years, he never gave her a key to his place. He didn't want her just dropping by. He considered her too much of a threat to all of his other games. He didn't like drama even though he was walking a thin line between Marti and having his ass hemmed up.

Marti was a computer engineer at IBM and she didn't care that he was a blue-collar worker because Marti loved her some V. Besides, he was making more money than she was. But V had a gift of gab that made the ugliest sister feel special.

Geena called to see what time I left for work. She said she wished she could have gotten some early morning lovin'. She was at work now. She had a mid-day wash and set. She wanted to rent some movies and chill at my house later. I told her I would call her and let her know. She seemed a little disturbed by that and hung up on me.

The phone immediately rang. I answered the phone with a little hesitation, "Hello."

"What's wrong with you?"

It was Sandy. She was talking like nothing happened last night.

"What was that all bout?"

"What? We've just started talking."

"Don't play me. That shit last night."

"What shit? Geena's a nice...."

"Why are you fucking with me, Sandy?"

"Cause you have been fucking with me for three years. Naïve little doctor chick, huh? She wouldn't know the difference."

"What about you and Mr. Universe?"

"I have never lied to you about anything. You knew I was dating other people. But my dumb ass never knew you were always dating other people even when I thought we were supposed to be exclusive."

There was a long pause. Dead silence. Someone could have broken out in an old negro spiritual. I didn't have anything to say. At least nothing sharp enough to cut as deep as she just cut me. I got it. I was about to break her butt down. Tell her how perverse this relationship really was and where she could stick it.

"Baby I love you. Don't do this to me."

"Do what? Be honest with you?"

"You know we don't have to go out like that."

"Go to hell."

She hung up.

I was about to give her a piece of my mind and I was catching nothing but dial tone.

Fuck her. I ought to go over to her house and show my ass. I caught myself. What am I doing? Had I lost my mind? Has this woman soaked into my spirit so deep that I couldn't shake her? Fuck her. Fuck her. Fuck her.

"Can I see you in my office?"

"Huh?" I didn't notice that Johnson had crept up to my cubicle. I wondered if he heard me and Sandy's conversation.

"Can you give me about five minutes, sir?"

"Yeah sure. See you in five."

I had heard that job cuts were coming soon. The firm hadn't had it so good since Dubya got into office. I had been making recommendations for the last two years about cut backs and layoffs at other companies and now my turn had come. I gathered my composure and headed to Johnson's office.

"How are you doing?"

"Come in. Sit down."

I proceeded and readied myself for the bad news.

"I love the job you've been doing for me and the company wants to promote you to Project Manager."

"What?"

"You heard me. This is a promotion. Thanks for the good work you've done."

"Thank you, sir."

"Don't be so hesitant. The job is yours."

Whoo. That was the best news I had heard all day. It was a good ending to a stressful day. I was going home. I was the boss. I could use some time off.

6 . . .

I came home and fell out. After what seemed like hours, I was awakened by a noise in my living room. "What the..." I didn't recall letting anyone in. What time was it? I looked at the clock. It was 8:30 p.m. I grabbed my bat from the corner and proceeded through the door like Walking Tall. Sleepy and all, I was ready to defend my domain. I was startled to find Geena sitting on my couch, drinking a glass of Chardonnay and looking at a rental copy of Love Jones. Her behavior told me that she was unfazed by the bat in my hand.

"I see you're up."

"How'd you get in?"

"You left the door open."

"I did?"

"I thought you left it open for me."

"Whatever."

I was starving. I hadn't eaten today. I walked in the kitchen. I noticed a bag on the day bar.

"What's this?"

"I got some rib tips from J.J.'s. I thought you might be hungry."

Damn. Geena knew how to look out for a brother. She stopped at J.J's Rib Shack and got me some rib tips. She was my girl. I grabbed a glass of Moss Bridge, my tips and sat down next to Geena. I would have been mad about Geena letting herself into my apartment but those ribs made up for that. Love Jones is our favorite movie. She enjoyed the movie. I enjoyed Nia. It had gotten to my favorite scene, the part where Larenz tries to talk Nia out of her panties when she makes him sleep downstairs. Just as Lorenz started to sneak upstairs, the phone rang. Not in the movie, at my house.

"Hello."

"Whatcha doing?" The voice on the other end asked.

It was Sandy. She was usually at the hospital at that time. Sandy worked at Grady Hospital. It's the County Hospital for Fulton and Dekalb Counties. She worked 6 p.m. until 4 in the morning. That was a large reason why I had been able to separate Geena and Sandy.

"Uh, nothing."

"I called in sick. Can I come over?"

"Over? Umm, not tonight."

Geena looked at me with a peculiar expression. She motioned her lips, "Who's that?" I had no choice but to come clean. I covered the phone and whispered back, "Sandy."

"What's up Sandy?!"

"Who is that?"

I was caught up. Drama. Drama. Drama.

"Your girlfriend is over there. I thought it wasn't serious. You are such a liar. I'm on my way over there."

Sandy slammed down the phone. I knew she was serious. She was an impulsive sister. That's what I loved and hated about her. I looked over at Geena. She was cussing Larenz out.

"He is such an ass... with his fine self." She laughed.

"Check this out. Let's get out of here. Go see a movie."

"What movie? We have one right here."

"I've been cooped up in here all day. I need some fresh air."

"Okay.   As long as you don't renig on the lovin'
tonight."

"I got you girl."

I got my ass out of there fast. I didn't know if Sandy was
coming for real or not. But I wasn't waiting around to see.
After the movie, we went back to Geena's house. I couldn't
believe this. In a matter of days, I had gone from smooth
operator to straight buster. I didn't know where it all went
wrong. But I had a feeling any good luck in my future was
going to be limited in a big way.

7 ...

I got up *Saturday morning*, dressed in my best NBA gear and headed down to the 'Run 'n Shoot'. As I passed the Gold Rush and Club Nikki, I reminisced of the days when I was sneaking into the clubs along strip club row. Atlanta has long been considered the sin city of the south, a lot of it remains in anonymity because of the right-wing bible belt enthusiasts that want to refrain from airing our own dirty laundry.   It's like my mama used to say...don't go in the street discussing family business.

I got to the gym. I could hear V hollering across the floor already. He was arguing against a travel called against him. V always traveled. I was used to it and tired of arguing. It was comical now. I shouted across the floor.

"Give up the ball!"

"I ain't giving up nothing!"

V noticed me.

"What's up dog! My dog is here now. We are about to run some stuff. Ya'll punks are through."

V and I grabbed some pick-up games on the far courts. We were in our early thirties and we lived on Tylenol and Ben Gay. We didn't dare touch the games on the right courts. Those were for the 'big dogs, the young dogs.' There were several brothers that could have played in the NBA, but lack of education and exposure had stymied their future. We ran the table 9 out of 10 games on the 'old dogs', and then watched the Summer League bruhs for about an hour.   We talked and caught up as we watched.

"Put that shit down, dog!" V referred to the brother that had slammed on the three others guys. "That's what I'm talking about. That's the way I used to do it."

"Man, you have never done that shit."

"Against George High in 84."

"Okay, V...You truly have a way of embellishing a story."

"You don't remember that?"

"Neither do you."

"Whatever man."

V got serious for a minute. I never saw V serious. He always had jokes. I think that's why we've had such a good relationship. I never recall us falling out. Ever. That's strange as I think about it now.

"Bruh, we're getting older right."

"Yeah", as if to say, where are you going with this?

"Take a look at this." V reached into his gym bag.

V handed me a small box. I stared at it with disdain. It couldn't be what I thought it was.

I opened the box. Damn, it was. It was an engagement ring.

"You ready for this man?" I asked.

"I love her. She gonna leave me if I don't do the right thing."

"What's the right thing ..."

"She's pregnant."

"Pregnant. You sure?"

"Yeah."

V sat there staring at the courts. He appeared very uncertain of his future.

"Look V. It's your decision. If you don't want to do it, don't."

"Yeah I know. But you know I don't want my child to

be a bastard. I want my kid to know I love him and his mother too."

I nodded my head with approval.

"If that's what you want to do. I'm here for you."

"Thanks bruh. I got a best man, right?"

"You Knowww!!!!! So, Marti already said yeah?"

"I haven't asked her yet."

"Well how do you know she'll marry your black ass?"

We laughed. We watched a couple more games and broke for home.

I had never seen V like he was that Saturday. Serious. Noble. He was going to be a father. I was going to be an uncle, a godfather. It made me think about what was going on in my life. I did some soul searching on the way home. When was the single life going to end for me? When was I going to get the pickett fence, the dog, the wife, and the kids? I had suddenly trapped myself with the big question and I didn't even have a candidate. What was that all about? Was I being truthful with myself or caught up in V's self-proclamation?

Those questions plagued me all day. I needed answers. My mind wouldn't rest until I had some solace to the confusion. I went home and pulled out the gray four-button suit, light gray shirt, and the steel colored tie. I needed to be close with the Lord. Geena volunteered to escort me in my search for answers. But she couldn't begin to understand the scenarios that were running through my head. Geena once proposed to me, but I couldn't do it. The time wasn't right. Now my boy was doing it. I would be on this island by myself. An island that I may or may not be able to handle as a castaway.

8 . . .

Geena and I decided to go to 9:45 service at my church, Jackson Memorial. Geena attended New Birth Baptist Church in Decatur, but I could pick her up and hit church in one swoop. Besides, I would be home for the Falcons game at 1. Geena was my road dog though. She was fearless. She was down with whatever. She would try anything once. I never went to church during football season. Asking her to go to church with me in September was unheard of. She never even asked why. It was what I needed. Seeing the old man leading the hymn stirred my soul. There were a lot of emotions I was feeling now. They overflowed like a gumbo during Mardi Gras. I couldn't tell the corn from sausage or the shrimp from the beans.

When Reverend Sutton called worshipers to Alter Call, I grabbed Geena's hand and pulled her to the front. I don't know what Geena prayed about. I needed answers. As I walked to the front, my mom's voice ran through my head over and over again.

"You need to go to church. Stop praying at home. Prayers are answered quicker in the Lord's house. He wants you to dedicate some time to him. He wants you to tithe. You need Jesus. Baby, please visit a church. I don't care which one. Just go."

My father never went to church, but my mother loved the lord.   She wouldn't miss a fellowship for anyone or anything in the world. She would wake Kareem and I up early on Sunday morning, fit us into leisure suits, turtlenecks, or a dress shirt and a clip-on tie and we would be off to fellowship. We were her road dogs, at least on Sundays anyway.

I held Geena's hand tightly at Alter Call. I don't know what she thought. I never told. She never asked. I prayed for peace and direction.

"Lord, please forgive me for my sins. I know I've been a sinner, but I kneel before you and ask for your forgiveness. Let me start by saying, thank you for blessing V and the decision he has made.   Let me thank you for giving me loving parents and a good life. Lord, give me the strength to change the things that I can change, the knowledge to recognize the things I can't, and the wisdom to know the difference. I ask you for some direction in dealing with the women in my life. I know, Lord, that you will only reveal things in their due time. But I ask for some light. Some guidance. Do I start fresh or do I take the hand of one of the women that is presently in my life? Lord, please give me a sign? Please show me a way. You are my rock. I can't and won't be successful without the power of your glory. Thank you, Jesus. Amen."

Geena and I rose up, left Altar Call, and went back to our pews. I looked around at my fellow worshipers. I felt so insignificant. They looked as though their problems are so much more important than mine and how dare God answer my petty trivial problems when there are people in this world with no food, no clothes, and are homeless. I had a whole lot to feel blessed about and probably took much of it for granted. With so much going on in the world, I was willing to be patient and let the important prayers be answered first. Like I had a choice.

Church service ended about 11:30. We rode home, but

there wasn't very much conversation. A lot of thinking was going on. Geena broke the silence.

"Do you want to go brunch at the Shark Bar?"

"Naw, the game comes on in a minute. I want to see the start of the game."

"Whatever. Drop me off at home."

"Why? What are you going to do?"

"I'm going to brunch at the Shark Bar." She snapped back at me.

"By yourself?"

"I thought I had a date, but obviously I don't. You know as much as I try, a lot of the time I feel like I'm in this game by myself."

I wondered to myself, "Where is she going with this?"

"What do you mean?"

"I'll tell you what. Think about it and get back to me."

"Geena, come on let's talk."

"I don't want to talk. I want to eat and listen to some gospel."

My head fell in my lap. I wasn't sure what I wanted to do. I wanted to accompany her. I also wanted to see the Falcons and Steelers. I had a split second to make a decision. We arrived at Geena's house.

"Well I'll be at home. Call me when you get back. We'll do something tonight."

Geena got out of the car without saying a word. No see ya. Goodbye. Kiss my ass motherfucka. Nothing. She never looked back as she walked into her house. The Lord had not answered any prayers about my confusion. After all, I did say I was willing to wait. I couldn't get Geena's behavior out of my head. I felt something was going on with her as well. She was going through an inner struggle. She had never acted that way. Not during the breakups. Never. What was her deal? I stopped at the Honey Baked Ham store on Riverdale Road and bought a fifteen-pound ham. Football game and ham sandwiches. Oh yeah.

About an hour later, I heard the guys upstairs joshing and joking about the game. I wanted to go up but I thought Geena might come over after she left the Shark Bar. Or maybe she didn't even go to the Shark Bar and was coming over for ham sandwiches. I stayed in the apartment. The afternoon light faded. No Geena. Mike called about 6:30. He was inviting me over to his house to watch the Sunday night game on ESPN. I declined, telling him I had to be at work early. He also congratulated me on the promotion. Even though it hadn't been formally announced, my promotion had spread through the firm like wild fire.

About two hours later, I was watching the game alone. The phone rang. I jumped over the couch to answer it. That was my baby's ring. Geena, not Sandy. It was V. He was calling to say he had made reservations for a dinner party on Friday at the Sun Dial Restaurant downtown and I was invited with a guest. He tried to get me to tell him who I was coming with, Sandy or Geena? I didn't tell him. Because frankly, I didn't know. We stopped to talk about the game several more minutes then shut it down. I told him I would see him on Friday. We really didn't hang as much as we used to. We had two different careers and different challenges to our everyday lives. He got paid for forty and overtime. I got paid for forty whether I worked forty or sixty. V had been in the assembly plant so long, the notion of working sixty hours for a forty-hour paycheck was absurd.

Neither Geena nor Sandy called me on Sunday night. Eventually I went to bed. About 1 a.m. I got up and called Geena. I don't know if she knew, but her behavior worried me.

Three days earlier, I probably would not have cared if she told me she was leaving forever. It would have just cleared a path for a relationship with Sandy. But I had a heart, I didn't want it to end like this. I was 31 years old. I've known Geena since the eleventh grade. It would have been a waste to end our interaction like this. Fuck that, I wasn't going to end it like this. But then again, was I paranoid or just overreacting? In reflection, it was probably a little bit of both.

Fuck it, I'm calling. The number was ringing. No Geena. I called again. This time I hung up. I guess I must have been afraid of the consequences. But what were the consequences? I asked myself if Geena was looking at the caller ID and decided she was never answering my calls again. What if another brother answered the phone and told me this was his territory now and he had everything under control, or somehow Geena and Sandy had talked and my whole life was now an open book. I could try to line them up in matter of importance, but frankly it didn't matter. All of them would suck.

I laid my head on the pillow. I looked up as the clock rang 1:45. I got up the nerve and called again. Her answering machine picked up.

"Geena...Geena, you there? For real Geena, pickup...please? Alright then you don't have to pickup, I'm gonna just say what I have to say. Look Geena, really if you are there pickup. I don't want to talk to a machine. Well, you're probably not at home. But it's 2 o'clock in the morning. Where the hell are you?! Okay, I'm going to say what I got to say. I acted like an ass this afternoon. I should have gone to the Shark Bar. After all, it was your treat." I laughed. "But seriously, I haven't talked to you all day and I'm worried about you. You got out of the car today, no goodbye, no nothing. Just hit me up when you get this message. I'll talk to you tomorrow, baby." I hung up.

Was it over the top? Probably, but desperate times call for desperate measures. I needed to do a little something extra. I got on the computer and ordered roses to be delivered at her shop. I thought it would help my position. I signed the card....'Mi amor siempre' meaning I love you always in Spanish. Geena's favorite language.

9 . . .

The next morning & decided to drive my truck to work. It was a beautiful day and I couldn't wait until Geena received her flowers. I worked hard to finish my analysis and cleared my calendar for lunch. I knew Geena would be calling any second. 12:30 came. No call. 1:00 came. No call. I called 1-800-Flowers to see if the flowers were delivered. They were delivered. Geena Gordon signed for the 10:25 delivery. I hung up the phone. Why no call? Damn, all this cause I wouldn't go to the Shark Bar? She was tripping and I needed to let her know. I went to lunch about 2. But instead of choosing a close restaurant, I decided to drop by Geena's salon.

The salon was off of Greenbriar Parkway across from the mall and next door to Burger King. I always thought the area was congested. But not today, Burger King was in the right spot.

I stopped by the salon mid-afternoon, but Geena wasn't there. Her stylists said Geena went to lunch about an hour ago. I asked them did she like the flowers? I got an overwhelming, "Yes!" That brightened my day. I grabbed a Whopper and headed back to work.

I checked my messages when I got back. There was no call from Geena, but Sandy did leave a message. I called her back. She called to apologize for the other night. She said

she didn't come over Friday evening. It was cool 'cause my
ass was out of there anyway. She wanted me to meet her for
dinner later. She was having a cold cut dinner at work and
didn't want to eat alone. I told her that I would stop by
about 9 o'clock. I was visiting my parents after work. She
said she would expect me then.

I decided to surprise 'Moms'. I hadn't seen her in two
weeks. We hadn't totally gone without communication.
We usually talked a couple of times a week. I told her
Geena and I went to church on Sunday. She was excited
about that. I didn't tell her I had a circus of things going
on with Geena and Sandy. My mother knew both women.
Both had been to my parents' house for dinner. My mother
didn't care, but my father liked Sandy better. I'd always had
aspirations of running for public office and he thought
Sandy was a better fit for my public image. My dad was a
good guy. Even though he never said it, sometimes I got the
impression that he had a skin color bias. I'm not saying he
did or didn't. I just felt that way. My family still lived in
the house I grew up in. We lived in the Sandtown
community. It wasn't Cascade Heights, but we held our
own. I grew up in the days where little league baseball and
football were king for a 12-year-old boy. Somehow, 20
years later, computer generated sports would steal the
energy from the real thing. As I think back, the 70's were
a good time. Our parents' generation inaugurated 'Super
Bowl' and 'Spades' parties. I remember my mother
allowing me to get up in front of her friends and relatives to
demonstrate that I had mastered the most recent Michael
Jackson and James Brown moves. I remember it so vividly.
"Look at my baby dance! Ya'll don't know nothing 'bout my
baby." That seems so long ago, yet it was still imprinted on
my soul.

When I hit the door, I could smell the good cooking.

"Hey Momma. What's up?" I said as I walked up
behind her.

I stopped for a second to take in the aroma of her spaghetti with sautéed mushrooms. She stopped cooking to give me kiss, "What are you doing here?"

"Trying to sneak up on you."

"Listen to you. You want something to eat?"

"Naw, I'm getting fat."

"I don't care. If you're hungry, eat."

"What's D up to?"

"I don't know. He was in the basement sawing. Probably trying to assemble something we don't need, as usual."

I sat at the breakfast table and talked to her as she cooked. I picked up the family photo album sitting on the armoire in the corner. We talked as I flipped through the pages. I'd looked through that book a thousand times before. What a fine woman she was back in the day. I could picture my dad in his frat colors barking at her across the campus, trying to get her attention. When I was little he used to say, "Boy you should have saw your mother. She used to be a hammer." Now her Cola bottle figure, long brown hair, and toned thighs had been replaced by an extra 30 pounds, a salt and pepper 'do', and a pretty chubbiness put on by marriage, happiness, and security. They were so comfortable with each other that my dad had an unconscious habit of walking around the house rubbing his stomach. Why? Because it was there.

I looked at my mom and wondered if she could measure the amount of childhood grief I'd given her growing up, and would she do it all over again. I don't think my mom and dad had an easy life. But if you asked her, she'd say it was a good life. It has been full of character. Character was something that she's big on. She demanded it. She would tell me from time to time that there were two things nobody could take away, my education and my character. As I looked in her face, I was ashamed of my behavior and the character I was displaying right now. As close as we were, she wasn't going to find out about this. This was going down like an ancient Chinese secret.

"V is getting married."

"Really? When?"

"I don't know. He hasn't proposed to her yet."

"Is it Marti?"

"Yeah."

"I like Marti. He deserves her."

"Yeah. I like her too."

My dad came upstairs at that time. He kissed my mother. I'm glad they still have love for each other after all these years. Something I want when I finally decide to tie the knot. My father looked at me, "What's up little man?" "What's up 'D'." That was short for daddy. I went straight from 'da da' to 'D.' He has called me 'Little Man' for as long as I can remember. He's always referred to me and anybody else as his little man.

"What going on in the consulting world?"

"I got a promotion."

"That's what I'm talking about."

"Make that money, son."

"See you can make a little money without a grad degree in your generation. It wasn't happening back in the day."

I remember when my father was in grad school getting his MBA. He spent many a nights studying right next to me. He would say, "Get your books Little Man. It's time to do some homework." We would go to the family room and study together. I was glad when he graduated so I could get a break. My parents and I laughed and joked. I didn't eat dinner, but I did have a piece of the honey butter Italian bread she made with her spaghetti. It was good, as usual.

I left my parents house and headed back downtown to meet Sandy for dinner. I arrived at Grady Hospital about 8:45. Before I got out of the car I checked my voicemail messages. I checked all of them. Cell phone. Work. Home. No Geena. I kept wondering what I had done to make her act like this. I cut my phone off before I went into the hospital.

I had been thinking about the situation all day and I was going to break it off with Sandy. As much as I thought I loved her, I had to let her go. The relationship was unhealthy. It was affecting my sleep, my job, and a part of my life I held sacred, my sanity.

I walked into the hospital. I thought I was going to have to go to the trauma center to meet her but she was in the vestibule as I walked in. Sandy actually was in residency at Emory, but she did her practical work at the Grady Trauma Center.

"How are you?" She said.

"How...are... you?"

"Are we imitating each other?"

I said, "No, I'm good."

"Let's go to the cafeteria. They have good subs."

We walked down to the cafeteria. We talked a little, but never really made eye contact. I let her walk a little ahead of me so I could savor what I would be missing.

I got the impression that I was gonna be missing a lot. Her presence caught the eye of every patient, visitor, male nurse, and doctor en route. I always got the impression that Sandy never noticed the attention she was getting. But she had to. It overwhelmed me. I was ready to fight the patient talking shit with the broke leg. She just kept walking.

"Did you hear that guy?"

"What guy?"

"The one that talked about your ass."

"No."

"Are you serious?"

"I didn't hear anything."

I left it alone. I came to realize that guys had been stepping to Sandy since she was 13 years old. She had learned to tune out shit that was unimportant to her. We ordered our sandwiches and found a set of chairs close to the door. Sandy wanted to make a quick exit just in case there was an emergency. I broke open conversation. After all, I needed to do this. Geena was going to be my girl and that's the way it had to be.

"So to what do I owe this invite?"

"I wanted to talk to you about the madness that's been going on with us and especially over the last couple of days."

"Me too. I wanted to talk to you about that also. Let me go first."

I wanted to go ahead and get it out. I needed to do it now. This was probably going to be the last time I would see Sandy. I looked sadly into Sandy's eyes and thought to myself, "Baby, I'll see you on the other side." Before I could start talking, she said, "No...no. Let me go first." Some men's weakness was food, for some, gambling, others, alcohol. Mine was Sandy, and as usual I caved in and let her go first.

"Go ahead."

"Well, I've been thinking. Doing some soul searching."

"Me too."

"I was thinking. We can't go on like this. It's just not healthy..."

She was rambling and about to one up me. She was quitting me before I could quit her. What a bitch. I had to get her first, so I interrupted her.

"Look Sandy."

"How rude. Let me finish."

"No. I really need to get this off my chest."

"I was talking."

"I know..."

"Will you let me talk?"

Damn. She was going to beat me to the punch. I couldn't let it happen. I jumped in again.

"Sandy."

But she just jumped in and said it.

"I don't want to lose you. I won't see Kevin anymore."
She got it out.

"Now, what did you want to tell me?"

After I soaked in Sandy's words, the breaks went on like an automobile screeching through a four-way intersection.

"I was saying...Baby, you're all I need."

"What are you going to do about Geena?"

"I think that's over." I said.

"Think?"

"It's over."

"Don't tell me what I want to hear.   Finish the relationship."

I agreed to.   Now I was at a point that I hoped that Geena wouldn't call so I wouldn't have to go through the drama.   Sandy walked me to my truck and gave me a deep kiss good night.   We were starting anew.   This was the commitment I had been waiting for. I arrived home about 11.   Instinctively, I checked my voicemail as I do each evening when I got home.   One call was V. The other was Geena.

"We need to talk. Give me a call when you get this message."

I began doing my best Florida Evans imitation, "Damn! Damn! Damn! I couldn't win." I decided not to call Geena that night.   I would get some sleep and call tomorrow. I slept good that night, for some unknown reason. I felt peaceful even though I was going through straight drama. Sandy called to wake me up and wish me a good day.

10

I got to work early. I wanted to make a good impression my first week as the boss. For the most part everyone was receptive except Dave. He was up for the promotion as well. I felt his energy and could tell he was a little bitter I got the job over him, but life isn't fair. Life is life. I decided when we had time I would pull Dave to the side and work out our issues. I had hoped we would still be boys, but that was up to Dave.

As the week went on, Geena must have called twenty-five times between home and work. I ignored them all. I didn't know what to say. I thought of a few things, "Babe you're out of here...I can't do this anymore...I need some space." That would have definitely given me away because she would have picked up that I had already made space. I had so many things going on right now, new job, Geena, Sandy, Dave. What else could happen?

I was completing a meeting in my office on Thursday afternoon, when I received a phone call. It was Kirsten, my little brother Kareem's girlfriend. He had been in a bad car accident and she couldn't reach my parents. Kareem moved to L.A. after graduating from North Carolina A&T three years ago. Kareem and I had been pretty close, but we had grown a little distant because he continued to call home and ask my parents for money to support his struggling acting career.

My parents had seemed satisfied with Kareem's progress. Me, on the other hand, thought Kareem needed to get a job. Wait a table, customer service, something.   He was just chillin', waiting on his monthly check from Mom and D. I never asked what his allowance was, but it must have been decent.   Kareem had a nice little apartment off Adams Boulevard in south-central Los Angeles.   He had gotten an internship at 100.3, The Beat Radio.   The internship allowed him to keep an inside ear on the happenings in the entertainment industry when he didn't have an acting job. His manager at the radio station allowed him the flexibility to schedule his job around his auditions. But that job barely bought him three meals a week. If he wasn't in the industry, he wanted to feel like he was close. Every once in a while, they allowed him to go on location and come on air with the Street Team.   He asked Kirsten to record him on-air so he could send a copy home to my parents.

My mother and father went on a cruise to Jamaica earlier in the week. I sent them a wire telling them what happened and not to make any moves regarding Kareem. I would call and give them some info when I got to L.A.   I let Johnson know about Kareem and grabbed the first open flight out of the ATL. I called Sandy and told her. She wanted to go but I decided to ride this one alone. She wanted me to call if I needed her, and she would take the flight out.

I had a three and a half hours flight and had plenty of time to think back about how we had harassed and supported each other over the years. When I was thirteen and Kareem was nine, my father would toss the football with us in the backyard for an hour before dark. After my father went in the house, Kareem wouldn't want to stop. At nine years old, this little boy would make me throw him a hundred passes. He was aiming for perfection at nine. Mosquitoes would be tearing me up. Him too, but he was still counting those passes. I could still picture him saying

"Ouch! These mosquitoes are tearing me up! Throw the ball." The boy thought he was invincible. Thank God there was no West Nile virus back then.   Kareem was an All-MEAC football player for A&T and had graduated in five years with a degree in electrical engineering. He was a smart guy. That's why we were so surprised when my brother said he wanted to be an actor and he was heading to Cali. During his senior year, he signed up for an acting class to trying to get close to a female drama major when the acting bug bit him.

When I was fifteen, I thought that I wanted to become a barber so I borrowed my neighbor Jeff's clippers. But I had no customers. I had to have a customer to practice my new profession. The perfect idea came when I saw my eleven year old little brother strolling to the refrigerator for a cup of Kool-Aid. Kareem's afro needed a little trim and shape. By the time I finished, Kareem was going for the Michael Jordan look. Okay, it was a little before Mike. Let's go with Isaac Hayes. Which was definitely not cool for a sixth grader. That was the last butt whipping I ever received from my father. As I recall, it was more like a fight. …that I was not destined to win. There was one thing I did find out that day. My daddy ain't no punk. Our refrigerator still has the dent to prove it .

I arrived in Los Angles about 8:30 p.m. It was close to midnight Atlanta time and I felt like I had been up forever. Kirsten was supposed to meet me at the airport. I hadn't met her in person, so I stopped by my parents' house and grabbed a picture Kareem sent home last Christmas. LAX had people everywhere, similar to Atlanta's airport. I saw no one that looked liked the picture, so I kept walking. I ended up downstairs at the luggage carousel. As my bag came around the carousel a beautiful lady called my name. I backed up and thought hard about how I knew the creamy skinned little sister? Her face didn't ring a bell, yet whoever she was, her round booty and pleasant spirit told me that she was someone I needed to know. Then she said, "They just moved Kareem from critical to stable." I thought to myself without even showing any emotion, "Oh Damn! You're Kareem's girl."

"Kirsten?"

"Yes. I recognized you from the photo album at Kareem's house."

"Really. I had your picuture and you don't look the same."

"My hair was shorter then and I've lost about 15 pounds."

I had to admit my little brother had taste. The sister was fine. I'm talking about top ten.

We loaded my bags in her rickety red Corolla and headed to the hospital. Kareem was being held at Cedar Sinai in Beverly Hills.

I hated this was my first time in L.A. and I was visiting on such a low note. Kirsten headed up Century and jumped on the 405 freeway. I was somewhat skeptical about that. I had heard the 405 traffic was like a parking lot. But it was pretty cool. L.A. had a nice breeze for a September evening but I couldn't get Kareem out of my mind. Was he going to be okay? Was he going to die? I don't ever remember my brother having the flu and now he was in Critical Care. It was hard to swallow. Kirsten scooted off the 405 and jumped on to the 10 freeway. She got off on La Cienaga and headed north. I was relieved when Kirsten told me he was stable. I was heading into the heart of Hollywood under such distressing circumstances. But it seemed as though I was sad and excited at the same time.

Kirsten and I didn't talk much on the drive to the hospital. She could see I was kinda zoned out. She was a little frazzled herself. She talked about the good times she and Kareem had, but I wasn't really responding to too many of her statements.

"We're almost there. Are you hungry?"

"A little."

"I'll call Jerry's Famous Deli for a pick-up order. It's across the street from the
hospital."

She made a call on her cellular and ordered us a couple of corned beef sandwiches to go. She asked me to go in and pick them up while she waited in the 'No Parking' zone. As soon as I got inside, I saw the brother who modeled for Polo in a booth off to the right. To my left, was the sister from 'Mad TV.' I kept my cool, but inside I was like "Damn!!!!!" I was very surprised to see the customers socializing, eating their meals, and paying little attention to the stars around them.

"Sir! Sir! Your order is ready."

"Oh! Oh! Thank you very much."

I grabbed our sandwiches and pushed through the small crowd as I headed for the exit. Kirsten and I were headed through the doors of the hospital about 12:30 a.m. Around that time, I got a call from Mom and D.

"Hello."

"Is my baby okay?"

"I'm heading into the hospital right now."

"Me and D are on our way."

"No. Don't do that? Kirsten just told me that they upgraded him so your coming may not be necessary."

"Let me speak to Kirsten."

It was almost one in the morning and I didn't feel like arguing so I just handed Kirsten the phone. I could tell by Kirsten's responses that my mom was prodding her pretty good, but Kirsten was holding her own and assured my mother that she would call her every 4 or 5 hours with updates. I think that calmed my mother. She didn't trust me. She always felt that Kareem and I had a competition to see who was the hardest and tonight that wasn't going to fly.

When we got to the Critical Care Unit, Kareem was

resting. I learned from the doctor that Kareem wasn't wearing his seatbelt when his car was hit. Kareem's head had hit the front window. The impact shattered the windshield and knocked him unconscious. The doctor said they were keeping him for 2 days because of a mild concussion and a bruised sternum. About 6 a.m., Kareem woke up with a headache. He whispered his girl's name.

"Kirsten."

I got up and walked over to the bed.

"She went to the bathroom bruh-man."

"What are you doing here?" He mumbled.

"Somebody had to come claim the body."

Kareem tried to sit up in the bed. I used my arm and pushed him back down.

"Don't tell me Mom and D came."

"Don't get up. Lie down and rest. Naw, they are waiting on me to give the word. But their bags are packed."

"I thought they were in Jamaica."

"They are."

"Call them and tell them I'm cool."

"Let me take care of that, you just rest."

Kristen came back into the room with 2 cups of coffee. She didn't notice that Kareem had woken up.

"Are one of those for me?"

"Kareem!", Kirsten shouted in a loud whisper.

She handed me the coffees and ran over and hugged Kareem.

"I was so worried about you."

"I see. You called my brother. You didn't have to worry about me. I'm Mrs. Douglass' favorite son. I ain't going nowhere."

When I heard that, my ears perked up.

"Yeah right. You ever heard of a seatbelt. They work you know."

"Hell, I was trying to put the damn thing on when that car hit me."

Kristen interrupted.

"Kareem, you never wear a seat belt."

"I was trying to put it on that time. I don't know why. Must have had a psychic premonition. "

"Yeah. Yeah. Man, get some rest. I'm about to call Mom and close my eyes for a minute."

I called my mother and let her know that Kareem was fine. She wanted to talk to him but he had fallen back asleep. I told her that I would call her when he woke up. They kept Kareem one more day and released him. He had some small headaches otherwise he was pretty good considering the circumstances. I spent the next week, keeping an eye on 'lil bruh and learning the sites around Los Angeles. I may have to come back and perpetrate like this was my adoptive city. Kareem and Kirsten took me to Mann's Chinese Theater in Hollywood, and Roscoe's Chicken and Waffles. I've got to say those were the best doggone chicken and waffles I ever tasted. I thought I'd do some shopping. After taking me to Fox Hills Mall, Kareem decided to take me to Del Amo Mall. When we got there, he asked me if anything looked familiar. I told him no. Why would I think anything looked familiar, I hadn't been to LA before.

"This is where they shot Jackie Brown."

"They sure did. There's the food court."

I remembered that. Kareem was in the food court scene, ordering a burrito or something. I picked up some items and we headed home. On our way, we headed down Artesia Boulevard. Before we got on the freeway, I noticed a fast food restaurant that had a line of cars wrapped around the building. I thought to myself, their food has got to be good. As we got closer, they sign seemed familiar. It was the Krispy Kreme. People were wrapped around the building like they were giving away a new car.

"Damn, what are they giving away at the Krispy Kreme?"

Kirsten laughed.

"Obviously, you've never tried Krispy Kreme's before."

"What? We got them on every corner in Atlanta. Like the way y'all have 7-11's."

Kisten looked at Kareem in her rear view mirror.

"You never told me that. You had me thinking we were trying something new."

"I didn't want to hurt your feelings. You were really enjoying that donut."

Kareem and I started laughing.

"Bruh. When Kirsten ate that donut, she was like, this is best damn donut I ever tasted. I didn't have the nerve to tell her that I grew up on them."

Kristen invoked the 5th Amendment and stopped participating in the conversation. But she knew it was all in good fun.

I screamed out, "Let's go to Venice."

When I hit Venice Beach, I knew I was in LA. The shops and street entertainers were just like they were on television. We stopped and watched a guy walk on glass and play a guitar at the same time. He deserved a tip. I walked out into the sand and let the breeze hit my face. I was in La-la. City of the Angels, baby. I thought of Biggie saying:

> *When La-la hits your lyrics still split ya*
> *Head so hard that your hat can't fit ya*
> *Either I'm witcha or against ya*
> *Format bent ya*
> *Back through the maze I sent ya...*

I smiled. "Going back to Cali. I made it Biggs." The women were not too bad either. I was blown away. I figured they could give the ATL a run for its money. But Atlanta was Atlanta and it's reputation for beautiful women would hold it's own with any major city. Kareem wanted to take me to the "Century Club." But he was in no shape to party. I told him I'd take a rain check. I think he was relieved.

I had a friend from college that had gotten a job at the headquarters of Honda America. I decide to call Tommy to see how he was enjoying life on the left coast. Tommy had married this psycho girl from undergrad, Felicia. They were now living in Long Beach. They invited me to dinner. I asked Kareem. He said it was about a twenty-minute drive down the 405 freeway. Kirsten dropped me off. After being in the room five minutes, I couldn't believe the wildest brother on campus was a married man with kids. Kids with Felicia at that. But the brother loved his life. He enjoyed his wife, kids and job, which was a little more than I could say for myself. I was going through some shit right now. I kept it all to myself. Nobody knew about my demons but me.

I talked to Sandy everyday. During my trip, she was my brick in the wall. She gave me a lot of emotional support. She had even volunteered to come to Los Angeles twice. I was very grateful but declined the offer. This was an opportunity for my brother and I to spend some quality time together. I also got nine or ten messages over the course of the week from Geena. She sounded like she was getting more and more irritated by me not responding to her calls.

I felt a little bad but then I thought, "fuck her." I tried to apologize by sending her flowers and she didn't respond to me. She could dish it out but she couldn't take it. Just so I wouldn't seem like a total jerk, I decided to give her call and leave her a message when I knew she would be at work. The phone rang and I was prepared to leave this sob story message when I got a ...

"Hello."

It was her. I hung up the phone I wasn't prepared to talk to her today and definitely not 2,500 miles away. When I hung up, I blocked the number just in case she tried *69. I was a grown ass man, playing these baby games. I felt like an idiot. But I was too far from home to argue with her. I had to live with my so-called guilt.

It was my last day in L.A. Kareem and Kirsten had shown me all the bubble gum stuff, now I wanted to go to the edge of L.A. Where the real happenings were, the NWA type stuff. They took me see the Watts Towers and Compton, which I didn't think was bad at all. Then we ventured to the Jungle. I told Kareem, I was looking for some edge. Not that much edge. We trekked back to the intersection of Florence and Normandy. The scene of where the '92 riots started. I was shocked. I would never have known it was the scene of a riot. It looked like a regular working class neighborhood in the ATL.

The next day, I said bye to my brother. Told Kirsten to take care of him and I got on a plane headed back to Atlanta.

CAUGHT UP IN THE RAPTURE

I arrived back in Atlanta and into the arms of Sandy who was waiting for me at the gate at Hartsfield International. She had flowers for me, which I thought was cool since I was usually the one giving the flowers. I was tired and wanted to go home. On the way, we talked about Kareem, Kirsten, my sight seeing ventures, and her job. She had a pretty good week and said she thought about me a lot. It made me feel special but I was too tired to express it.

When we got home, Sandy said she was going to make some tea. I didn't care. I took my clothes off and got in the shower. I leaned against the side of the shower and soaked my face in the water. Before I knew it there was another warm body in the shower, kissing my back. As tired as I was I turned around and was mesmerized by her green eyes. We embraced as I kissed her collarbone, moved down her shoulder and arms, and sucked her fingers. She moaned rolling her head back. We shared kisses. She kissed my chest and moved, taking small intense nibbles on my nipples. I wanted to scream. I missed this woman. We made love in the shower for what seemed like an hour. Then moved to the bedroom where we kissed up and down each other's backsides until exhaustion set in. We fell asleep hard. I don't know when I dozed off, but I woke just before the break of dawn to hear Sandy's peaceful little snore.

I got to work the next morning around 8 o'clock ready to take on the world. My family was okay, new promotion, had just gotten some good luvin'. Dave came by my cubicle, asked about Kareem and apologized for his poor attitude last week. I accepted and we agreed to have lunch before the week was out.

I was about halfway through the day and found myself staring at the phone. I needed to call Geena. She was on my mind. I had a quick meeting with Johnson. Came back and decided to call Geena. That was the slowest dial of my life. The number rang. It sounded like someone picked up but there was no hello, so I spoke first.

"Hello....Hello."

"So why now am I lucky enough to get a phone call?"

It was a pressure question. I knew I had to come back with something clever.

"I don't know what you are talking about?"

I could tell that didn't go over well. But I had to stick to my guns. She didn't respond...so figured I had the upper hand. I repeated myself a little bolder.

"What are you talking about?!"

"Just meet me at Sylvia's after work, nigga."

She hung up on me. All I heard was dial tone. I left the conversation feeling the control had shifted and frankly I didn't feel that cocky anymore. I felt uncomfortable for the rest of the day. I wanted to get to Sylvia's a little later than Geena so I could gage her demeanor through the restaurant window. I got to Sylvia's about 5:25. No Geena. My plan had unraveled, so I decided to go in anyway. I sat there for about thirty minutes and still no Geena. It had gotten dark so I couldn't see the outside landscape. I got the feeling that Geena was outside the restaurant watching and measuring my behavior just as I had planned to do her. I suddenly began to feel uncomfortable. I ordered a couple of Long Island Ice Teas and downed them as if they were

Lipton's.   I paid the waitress and approached the door.   As I was leaving...guess who comes through.   Geena.

"Where you going?"

"Home. You were supposed to be here at 5."

"So I am little late. Come on back in."

"I ain't going back in there.   I am about go next door to Kroger and get me a Hoagie and take my ass home."

"Go on back in."

"I said no!"

"Go back in the restaurant..."   She mumbled.

"What?!"

"Get your ass back in that restaurant!"

She kinda scared me but I followed her directions and went back in.   The waitress met us.

"Oh, so your party showed up.   I'll give you the same table."

I regained my composure so the waitress wouldn't sense any trouble.

"Thank you.   The lady will have a glass of white Zin."

"No that's okay.   I won't be having anything."

"What? You always drink white Zin."

"I said I didn't want any alcohol."

"Okay. Chill.   I was just being cordial."

"Cordial. Cordial.   That's what I get now, cordial? That's what I rate, cordial?"

"What's going on?   What's up with you, Geena?"

"Why didn't you call me back?   I know you got my messages."

"I did get your messages but I was in Los Angeles. Kareem was in a bad car accident.   He was in Critical Care."

I hated using my brother to rally sympathy, but I had to do what I had to do.

"Oh my goodness, Is he okay?"

"He's better.   It was give and take for a minute.   But he's a big boy."

"That's good.   I'll have to call him."

"So back to you. What's been going on with you?"

"I'm pregnant."

When she said that, it seemed everything in the universe just stopped and we were the only things moving. Nobody was in the restaurant, no traffic outside. Just us.

"You sure?"

"Yes I'm sure. I was going to tell you last Sunday after church."

Damn! My life had stalled again. What was really going on? My first thought was to follow the question mark stereotype that bestows a man uncertain of his future. I wanted to ask her, "Whose is it?" But I knew whose baby it was. I looked at the dignity in Geena's eyes and knew that was a question that would have been beneath her.

"Have you thought about what we're going to do?"

"What I'm going to do?"

As scared as I was I knew I had to show some allegiance and solidarity. Geena's hands were flush on the table. I put my hands on top of Geena's.

"No.....we."

I was hoping I was giving her some sense of security but I was confused myself. She told me three years ago that she couldn't have babies because of her fibroid tumors. So how was she pregnant now? Act of God? Act of Congress? What? I needed some answers. But this wasn't the time or place. Geena and I decided not to spend the night together. We went back to the car, we cried a little, laughed a little, hugged, and said goodbye for the night.

Geena decided that she wanted to make an initial decision and we could talk about it after. Over the next several days, Sandy could sense something was wrong but I wasn't letting on. I was just not acting myself. Sandy was having a get together at her house on Friday night and wanted me to come.

I got to Sandy's loft around 8:30. Sandy had the phattest loft. She stayed in Renaissance Lofts looking over

the Atlanta skyline.   She had cathedral ceilings and
hardwood floors. She had the bachelor pad. At least the
one I wanted if I could afford to live downtown.

When I got there several people had already arrived. I
got the impression pretty quickly that everyone in the room
had adopted themselves into the 'uppity' Negro club. I was
amazed at the different types of people Sandy had met in the
small amount of time she'd been in Atlanta. She'd invited
her doctor friends, and a lawyer or two. She had also invited
a few people from the bohemic set, two writers, a painter,
and poet. It was definitely an eclectic set. I didn't know
anyone, but a few seemed to know me. ...Or should I say...
of me. Sandy escorted me around the room introducing me
to several people. I was surprised I wasn't connected to any
of the people in the room. Afterall, I was born and raised in
Atlanta. International city or not, Atlanta was sort of a big
town and everybody was connected in some way.

About 10, there was a knock at the door. A familiar face
finally walked into the room. It was Michael Love. I ran
track with Mike in high school. Mike went to Michigan
and now he was a backup wide receiver with the Cowboys.
I was surprised to see Mike in a Cowboy uniform when
Dallas came to Atlanta for the Super Bowl. Mike never
played ball in high school.

We made eye contact immediately and embraced in a
brotherly hug.

"What's been going on?"

"Chillin. Just trying to make ends meet."

"But I see ends are meeting for you like a motherfucka."
I joked.

"I'm just trying to do my thang."

"I feel you. I thought you were supposed to be in
Dallas?"

"We're playing Atlanta on Sunday. I flew in a day early
to see my parents."

"How are they?"

"They're good."

"So who do you know here? My girl Sandy?"

I backed up for a minute but didn't show any emotion.

"Your girl Sandy?"

"Yeah. We were fucking when she was at Northwestern." He confided in me.   "We met at the Big 10 Track Championships. I laid wood to her the first weekend we met. I haven't seen her in minute. She's fine as all outdoors. Ain't she?"

"She is that."

"She's a smart girl, but she definitely has a little freak in her."

We looked at her across the room. I didn't respond.

Sandy never made her way over to Mike and I. I think she felt a little exposed. I never let Mike know that Sandy and I were closer than I let on. I didn't bring it up to her. I hoped she would talk to me about it, but she never did. I watched her as she made her way around the room.

On my way home, I noticed that Geena had left a message on voicemail saying she was lonely and needed someone to talk to. It was almost 3 a.m. now, I didn't call her. I figured by now she was probably asleep. I also got a call from Sandy saying that she would meet me at my house. It was too late to tell her no. She was already in route. We didn't make love that night. We just slept. Sandy didn't like to wear clothes to bed and neither did I for that matter. With everything going on with Geena, I didn't feel comfortable lying beside another naked woman, including Sandy. I kept on my boxers.

The next morning I got up and fixed Sandy and me some breakfast. I figured she would be gone around 2, I could watch a college game then call Geena. About 11, the phone rang. I answered it. It was V.

"Get up Man, you've slept half the day away."

"I'm up dog. I was fixing some breakfast."

"Who's there?"

"What do mean? Who's there?"

"You don't eat breakfast. Who you foolin'?"

"Sandy."

"Tell her fine ass, I said what's up."

"Hey! Hey! Don't be talking about my woman."

"I wonder where I've heard that before."

Sandy wrapped a sheet around herself and had moved to the couch in the living room. She was watching one of the teen shows on NBC Saturday. She wasn't paying attention to me.

"V says what's up!"

"Tell V, I said ditto."

"She says what's up."

"She's too cool. You need to keep her."

"I'm trying bruh. I'm trying."

V called to tell me that he was inviting us to a dinner party at the Sun Dial Restaurant on Friday. He was going to propose to Marti in front of their families. He wanted his boy to be there. I told him I would. But I didn't tell Sandy, frankly because I didn't know who I was taking to. Sandy or Geena. Sandy and I made love one time before she went to work. I was in a state of ecstasy and guilt simultaneously. She kissed me bye. I returned a half-hearted kiss. I wondered if Sandy had detected my standoffish behavior. She never mentioned anything.

About 3 o'clock, Geena called. She wanted to see me. She asked me to come over to her house. I told her I would be over around 6. I could have come sooner, but nervousness held me back. But I didn't know what to be nervous about. Her having a baby or her having an abortion? We were both in our thirties and childless. I knew I couldn't put my foot down and say have the abortion. That shit was out of the question. I took the long way around to Geena's house. My mind was going a hundred miles an hour. Would I be a good father? A terrible father? How would my dad's role in my life shape

my parenthood? If she got an abortion, would I feel guilty?
It was the longest drive.

Geena let me in.   The ambience of the house was
somber.   This was it.   I had made up in my mind that I
wasn't going to argue with her decision. I wanted to honor
it. She invited me to sit down. It seemed as though she
wasn't ready to speak so I spoke first.

"How are you?"

"I'm okay."

"Long time no see."

"That was on you. You knew where I lived."

"I was waiting on your call."

"You're always waiting on my call. What are we doing
here?"

"I thought I was coming over to talk about...."

"...What are we doing?

"Doing?" I pretended to get dumb.

 "As in you and me."

Now why did she have to ask me that? I wasn't prepared
for that question. That wasn't in the rules. I needed to say
something to stall the question.

"Where did that come from?"

"What do you mean where did that come from? It came
from wondering about the future of this relationship."

I thought to myself, "Damn! Why is she putting this
pressure on me?"

"I think..."

"You think. Eight years and you think."

When she said that, I grew livid. Who did she think she
was? She was trying to back me into a corner. I took a deep
breath. Swallowed.

"Okay. Okay. I've wanted out for the last two years."

"Why was I the last to know? You've been dragging me
along for the last two years knowing this relationship wasn't
going anywhere?"

"I tried to give you hints."

"Hints! Why couldn't you just be a man and tell me what you were feeling?!"

"I don't know! I don't know."

Geena laid back on the couch, covered her face, and began to cry. That's why I never said anything. This is what I had been avoiding. I wasn't ready for it, but the cards were on the table and I had to deal with it. I didn't know if I should console her. Not say anything? Or finish my story. I walked over to her side of the couch and sat next to her. I put my hand on her shoulder. Right then, right there I wanted to hug her, but the hand on the shoulder was a litmus test.

"Don't touch me! Don't ever touch me!

Well I knew she didn't need a hug at that point. I didn't want to say the wrong thing so I sat there stupefied. With the "What do I do now?" look on my face. I really had no warning as to what was about to happen next. The Geena from London Townhouses appeared from nowhere. She became a hard, arrogant, and defiant sister.

"I'm gonna have this baby."

"What? What do you mean, you're going to have the baby? Don't I have some say so in this?"

"You just had your say so."

"When?"

"When you started saying stupid shit."

"Look, I was just being truthful with you. Both of us should have a say in this."

By this time, I wanted her to have the abortion.

"Well I'm having this baby and I've got control over this. You can do whatever you want."

"You are on crack. I'm getting the hell out of here."

I got up and charged toward the front door.

"Yeah, you do that. ...And tell your girlfriend, Sandy, you're going to be a daddy."

I paused for a second. Everything went in slow motion when Geena said that.

12 . . .

I left Geena's house upset, mad, and confused. Upset that I had no say in her decision, mad that she would attack me like she did, and confused on how my game had been exposed. My priorities must have totally shifted because I concentrated more on the latter rather than the first. How did she know? When did she know? I had learned from my grandfather, who had been a renowned player. "When you're playing the game, you must understand that you'll win some and lose some. The fool is the one who thinks he will never be caught or he will win them all." I had lost one, but it was a big one. This was the one that could possibly never turn back the hand of time. But where did I slip and where was I exposed? These questions haunted me throughout the week and in my sleep. Geena and I didn't talk the rest of the week. Sandy was beginning to pick up on my behavior. I passed it off as being under the weather. I faked a sore throat and a few sneezes in between. But I knew I would have to tell the truth sooner or later. For the first time, I actually felt like I was leading a double life.

Sandy and I went to V's family dinner at the Sundial on Friday. The Sundial was a rotating restaurant that sat on the eighty-fifth floor of the Westin Peachtree Plaza Hotel. It was an exclusive yet trendy restaurant that towered above

Atlanta's skyline. V had reserved the dinner for 6:30. I thought the timing was bad considering rush hour traffic, but everybody showed. I decided not to go home after work. Sandy took a couple of hours off.

It actually turned out to be beautiful. We were seated just as the sun set in the west and the lights of Atlanta's skyline were absorbing what natural light was left in the east. V didn't choose this moment in time, it chose him. Just as everyone was finishing their dinner and good conversations were going on throughout, V asked the waiter to bring champagne and cheesecake. As he stood, I was wondering how was he going to get it out. I had known V since the fifth grade and frankly I didn't think he had it in him. He stood and prepared himself to address the party.

"I want to thank all of you for coming. My family, Marti's family, especially her dad, cause he doesn't come to nothing."

Everybody laughed. The waiter was serving the champagne.

"My boy and his girl came. Thank you man, I appreciate it."

I held up my glass and motioned, "No problem." He acknowledged a thank you back and continued.

"I asked you guys to come because frankly I love all of you and we need to get together sometimes. It shows us as one. I love that."

At the same time, Marti was reminding him of the thank you's he was forgetting. He cut her off in the middle of her sentence.

"Baby, you want to talk? Baby, it's your party too. You can say whatever you want to. I tell you what, why don't you just hold the toast! It's your party."

Everybody was rolling. Marti took the challenge, grabbed her glass and jumped up laughing.

"Vlad was just being silly. I'll hold the toast. There are times that are priceless and this is one of them. Especially when I see my daddy. I love you mom and daddy. I love you too Mr. and Mrs. Williams. This toast is not for me, it's for you. This is for your love, your guidance, and a thank you for being you."

Marti held up her glass and toasted. The crowd followed her lead. But all eyes were on Marti. As she brought the glass to her lips to seal the toast, she caught a flicker of something in her glass. She looked over at V.

"There's something in my glass." She gasped.

"What?" V asked.

She looked closer, it was an engagement ring. Marti collapsed in her chair and started crying. Her mom ran over to console her.

"Baby you okay?"

"I Can't believe this...Mom, you knew about this all the time?"

"Yeah I did. It was supposed to be a surprise."

"I should have known something was up. Daddy was here."

Everybody laughed. Marti's father then asked her a question.

"The brotha needs you to answer his question."

Marti shouted, "I haven't been asked a question."

The crowd continued to giggle. It was definitely a moment. V responded, "I tried to. You wouldn't shut up."

"You should have kicked me."

I laughed. They made the perfect couple.

"Marti, you have been with me during thick and thin. During good times and bad. I love you more than anything in this world and that will never change. I ask you here in front of my family, your family, the world, and God...Will you be my wife?"

Marti started to cry again, but didn't respond.

V said, "Baby, are you okay? Is everything alright?"

"These aren't tears of sadness, I'll tell you that. Yes Vlad. I would be honored to be your wife."

V cupped her face and kissed Marti in front of God and
the world. Sandy clutched my arm tight.   I looked in her
eyes and thought this could be me and you. All of a sudden,
I imagined Geena holding a baby over Sandy's shoulder.
    "Are you okay?"
    "I'm good. I was just daydreaming."
    "Daydreaming about what?"
    "Me and you girl. Me...and...you."
    "Yeah right. You are so silly. They make a beautiful
couple."
    "They do."
    A little bit later V pulled me aside. He asked me how
everything went.   I told better than he could have ever
planned. He said that over the last two weeks he had gotten
used to the idea of him becoming a dad.   Even though V
was with me at that time, I was still alone and my thoughts
were going a hundred miles an hour. I thought to myself,
here are two brothas who have been around each other their
entire lives. We were like family, the same values, the same
educational structure, but we were going in two totally
opposite directions.
    I was happy for my boy, jealous of my boy, and confused
about life.
    "Hey bruh. I need to ask you something."
    "Yeah man, go ahead."
    "I couldn't think of anybody I'd want to be my best man.
Would you?"
    "V, give me the time and the place. You know I'll be
there for you."
    "Besides, who could throw a better bachelor party?"
    We laughed, hugged and returned to the party.

13 . . .

I got a call from Geena on Saturday asking me to
come over. I had put the weekend on hold
hoping that Geena would call and recant her thoughts on
this baby thing. So when she called, I rushed over. On my
way there, I played a couple of scenarios in my head. Was I
supposed to be happy? Sad? Was I supposed to console her?
Would we cry together? After all, I wasn't proud of this. It
wasn't the feather in my cap. But Sandy wouldn't be very
accepting of this little hitch in the road.

I got to the house. It was dark. I rang the bell twice.
There was no answer. What was going on? I decided to use
my key. Geena had given me key a couple of years ago. I
rarely used it. I thought this would be good time since
Geena and I had business. I walked in slowly. It was dark.
What the hell was going on? If she came around the corner
with a knife or gun, I was gonna punch her like a man. I
wasn't going out like no sucker. This was sucker shit and I
was looking like a guinea pig with a big blow-pop.

"Is that you?"

I spoke up, "Yeah."

"I'm back here."

What did Geena have in mind? In the dozen years that
I had known Geena I had never been afraid of her
intentions. Right now....I didn't know what to expect.

I opened the bedroom door, she had on my favorite piece from page 34 of Victoria Secret's Christmas catalog. I thought to myself, "Damn!" But I kept my composure.

"Geena, what are you doing?"

"Be quiet."

She unzipped my pants, raised my shirt, and started kissing my stomach. I was trying to straighten up my life. This couldn't be right. I had to do something. I had to say something. After a couple of shouts of the "Holy Divinity." I was prepared to speak up and put a stop to this madness.

"Oh yeah, baby. Don't stop…Jesus….Don't… stop."

"You like this."

"Shit yeah! Why are you doing this to me?"

"You are my man. Aren't you my man?"

"Why are you doing this to me?"

"No?"

Ecstasy filled my body and was burning on overload.

"Baby I love yoooouuuuuuuu!!!!!!!!"

"You do?"

"I do. I do." I screamed. "Damn."

"I love you too."

I exploded. I had been leaning up against the wall and needed a seat. My heart was pounding so fast. I shimmied across the floor with my pants around my ankles. As I passed her, Geena smacked my ass so hard I flinched. I turned around quick. She stood there smiling as if to say you're my bitch and don't you forget it. I was confused. I didn't know if I was coming or going. Geena fell on my chest. She smelled so sweet. The Dolce & Gabbana she wore had filled the room and set an ambience for the evening. I had been seduced and couldn't deny I loved every minute of it.

"Get rid of her. We're the family."

"We're the family, baby." I mumbled as I fell into a deep sleep.

A couple of hours later, I awoke. I looked over at

Geena, she was still sleeping. Her stomach had begun to form a small pooch. Damn, she was starting to show. What was I going to do? What would Sandy say? I slipped out of bed, grabbed my clothes and put them on as I was making my way to the door. I eased out of the house. I tried to put my shoes on as I sneaked to my truck, but my big toe missed the insole. I suddenly stumbled and bumped Geena's car, the alarm sounded. As I studied the landscape, I saw light after light coming on in the neighborhood one at a time. Geena was up quick. She knew the sound of her alarm. She rushed to the door. She realized it was me and shut down the alarm.

"Where are you going?"

"I...I was getting something out of my truck."

"Oh. Well, hurry up and come on back in. I'm cold."

I faked it and got my Palm Pilot out of the truck. Geena's eyes escorted me to the truck and back into the house. Why was she eyeballing me? We had been dating all these years. Where was the trust? She disappointed me. I came back in like a puppy dog with my tail between my legs. I made my way back to Geena's bed, she cupped herself in my shoulder and fell off to sleep.

I awoke the next morning to the smell of Spanish omelets and pancakes. I mosied into the kitchen to get my half of the meal. I could already taste my omelet, bacon, and blueberry syrup. Geena was eating breakfast and reading the morning paper. I was stunned to see she didn't fix me anything.

"Where's my food?"

"What food?"

"My omelet."

"I didn't fix you an omelet."

"Why?"

"You didn't ask for one."

"Is that where we are now? I have to ask for food even if you are already cooking?"

She looked at me, shook her head and hsst, "...Yep that's pretty much it until you take care of your business." I got mad. As selfish as I had been in the past I couldn't believe she didn't fix me an omelet. I thought to myself, "What a bitch."

"Did you say something?"

She better chill. I know she didn't want me to raise up on her ass. Cause if I had to I would.

"No. I think I'll have some juice."

14 . . .

I got back to my house, took a shower, and got dressed for work. I had missed the 7:38 train so I decided to drive into the city. Halfway through my 15 mile-per- hour commute, I was cursing rush hour traffic and remembering why I caught the train everyday. I got to work about 8:40 and immediately started in on my workload. Kelly, the department clerk brought the reports that I requested the day before. As I looked around my office area, I started to inventory the personalities and mannerisms of my colleagues. They seemed to be peaceful, not a care in the world while mine was in total turmoil. But I had to keep my composure, set the example. I was the boss.

Mike came through. He had been on vacation and was stopping by to say hello.

"What's happening man?"

"What's going on? How was the vacation?"

"It was off the hook, man. I didn't want to come back."

"I feel ya."

"We hit the Caymans and Acapulco. The water was blue and bikinis and thongs everywhere and that was just on the boat."

We laughed.

Mike and I came to the firm about the same time. We had grown very close over the past four years. We had gone out several times. Me and my dates, Mike and Tonya, his wife. I always thought of them as somewhat of the odd couple. Mike talked a lot of trash, while Tonya was quiet and reserved. I always thought of Tonya when I heard girls describe themselves as "Cute in the face and thick in the waist." Tonya was straight beautiful. Probably one of the most beautiful women I had every seen, but she had put on about 40 pounds since they had gotten married. Mike was somewhat athletic. He was over six feet and a little over two hundred pounds. But it didn't matter how much weight she had put on. Mike loved that woman. You could tell. He worshiped her, every pound. They were three kids deep but the love was there as if it were the first day he told her he loved her. ...And she felt the same way about him. I joked with him once. I told him that neither one of them would ever leave each other. One was going to have to die first. He just laughed and said, "I know that's right. I ain't leaving her and if she left, I'd kill me." I thought his statement was somewhat bizarre but I admired that on the other hand. I wished I could be in a relationship where the love was bigger than life itself. They were good people.

We talked about some reports that were nearing deadline. We talked about a workshop that I had asked him to prepare and his approach to a new client. Mike always worked hard. I was always impressed with his knowledge of the job. He was my confidant at work.

"Let's go play 9 holes after work?" He asked.

"I really have some shit to do, but I guess I can squeeze in a 9."

"What you got to do? You ain't married."

"Just got a promotion. Look at my desk, you tell me. But yeah, I'll play. I need to go home and get my sticks."

"I keep mine in the back of the car. You got to be ready dog."

"I know."

My day went well, I managed to get through the day

without thinking about Sandy or Geena.

I met Mike at John A. White Park. It was a course near where I had grown up. I had an advantage on Mike. I knew the course. While in college on a track scholarship, I ran the fairways to get in shape for track season. It was up and down. Up and down. Running that course had almost burst my heart on several occasions and my driver was about to burst Mike's game this day.

Mike talked trash from the time we got out on the course. Neither one of us were very good. The pride came from beating each other. I lost 3 balls that day. Mike lost 2. Our game was filled with trash talk and insults, but both of us had thick skin and that's what made the game fun. Mike hit his shot.

"Who's the man!?"

"Now play the game, and let's leave your mama out of this."

"Oh. Oh. Let's get off of mamas. Let's get off of mamas. I just got off of yours."

As I hit the ball, I would say, "This is for Barbara Ann." That was Mike's mother. That would irritate him. His shot would be off like a light switch. It was cool to say mama, but don't start mentioning names. I think it set off a picture in Mike's mind. But it was cool. All was fair in love and golf. We talked trash, laughed, drank brew when Mike said something about his brother having his first child. The conversation sprang pictures of Geena in my head. Pictures that I couldn't let go. I did my best to keep my game, but I kept thinking about me, Geena, and the baby. I pictured us as a family. In the 8 years, I had never thought of me and Geena as family and not to mention other little people involved in the situation. I was a career bachelor and it was coming to a close. I just knew it.

Whether it being Geena or Sandy I was going to marry one of them. My days of bachelorhood were closing in fast. I needed to get the madness off my chest and Mike just happened to be at the right place at the wrong time.

"Mike."

"Stop talking dog. I'm trying to putt."

He missed the hole again.

"Naw, seriously bruh."

"What you need man?"

"Have you ever had two women and you couldn't decide which one you wanted?"

"Why decide? You ain't married."

"One is pregnant."

"Whewwww!!!!!! Which one?"

"Geena."

"She's fine bruh. What you gonna do?"

"I don't know. That's why I'm talking to you."

I shook my head bewildered.

"I can't believe this is happening to me."

"Why don't you just marry her?"

"What about Sandy?"

"Yep....She's fine too. You got issues."

He finished his putt.

"Is she going to have it?"

"She says she is."

At that moment, a golf ball almost busted Mike in the head. Mike looked back at the golfers behind us.

"Hey! What the hell are y'all doing?!

"My bad!" The guy hollered back.

"You need to holler 4 or something!"

I guess that was their way of telling us that we needed to move our asses on. We had been at the 5th hole talking for twenty minutes.

By the time we got to the 9th hole, I had shot 63 and Mike had shot 68. That was the equivalent of Tiger Woods beating us both by 50 strokes. We were terrible. We knew it, that's why we're consultants. We were in the consulting game.

We finished playing about 8:30. Mike headed home. I

headed to my mother's house.   Maybe she had cooked
dinner.   I got to my parents house, my mother's car wasn't
there.   I figured she worked late.   My father was there.   He
was in his domain.   He was in the backyard grilling burgers.
I walked around the house following the aroma.

"Hey old man, can I have a burger?"

"Sure. Pull up a seat."

I pulled up my father's favorite seat.   The one he had sat
in for the last twenty years.

"Not that one son. Pull up another."

"I thought you slipped D."

"Never son. Not getting old. Just getting better."

"I know. That's why those knees sound like firecrackers
going off."

I pulled up another chair and sat down for some father
and son bonding.   The aroma of my father's burgers had
christened the whole neighborhood.   Mr. Strozier, my
parents' next door neighbor, let my father know that he
wanted one when they were done.   I think he intentionally
over manicured his garden waiting on his burger.

"The council election is coming up soon son."

"I'm not ready for it yet, D."

"Son, we need to get this thing off the ground.   The
trust fund we set up for the campaign is getting old."

"I got issues of my own right now. I'll be ready for the
next one."

"What issues? Job is going well. You're attractive.
College grad. Son, we're ready for this. This is our time."

"I like the way you said that. Our time, huh?"

"Our time."

I thought this was a good time to feel my dad out, since
he was feeling me out.

"What do you think about grandkids?"

"They'd be good after a wedding."

My father suddenly stopped flipping burgers. My father
had a way of getting his point across without even looking

at you. He paused.

"Son, tell me I'm not thinking what I think I'm thinking."

"It's according to what you are thinking."

"Okay, Mr. Comedian give it to me straight."

I looked at my father and broke down. My expression said it all.

"Well, why didn't you use protection, Son.?"

"She told me she had fibroids."

He shook his head bewildered.

"Son."

"D, I don't know what happened."

"First of all, let's be truthful. You know what happened."

"I know I was irresponsible."

Hearing it from my dad cut short all the "Ata-boys" he had given me over the years. The baby would have been the first child in our family born out of wedlock. I had a lot of thinking to do. Throwing my hat into the political arena was on an indefinite hold for right now. My dad gave me a hug, gave me burger, then we talked about options. The possibility of him becoming a grandfather. He asked me how was Geena taking it. I told him the situation wasn't good. My father never delved into my personal relationships so I decided not to tell him that Sandy was also part of this web. That would have sprang a whole new conversation, one that I wasn't ready to explain. He said that he wouldn't tell my mother, that responsibility was on me. But he vowed to support me in whatever decision I made. I loved my dad.

I got home about 10:00, there were a few phone messages. Geena, Sandy and a couple bill collectors. The first one was Geena, "It's 8:00, where are you? I hope you are taking care of the business we talked about."

The next one was Sandy.

"What's up baby? We haven't spoke in a couple of days.

You act like you don't like me anymore. If I don't hear from you by tomorrow, I'm going to take the proposition from the guy on the 8th floor with the football helmet. Take care, handsome. We'll talk soon. Call me if you need your toes sucked."

She started laughing, "Bye boy. Talk to you later." I laughed with her.

I took a shower and stared at the phone. Who would I call first? Hell, it didn't matter. I was in a deep mess with both of them. I decided to get some sleep and call them the next day.

The next day when I got to work, I got a message from Johnson telling me to contact the Travel Department. Rich and I were going to see a client in Newport News, VA. I called travel and stopped by Rich's cubicle to see if he had gotten the message.

"Rich, you busy?"

"Not really. I was trying to line up some play from the receptionist in the lobby."

"You better leave those sisters alone. They're gonna hurt you."

I had come to the conclusion that Rich really thought he was black. I saw him a couple of weeks ago at Lenox. He was with Deidre. He was dressed in Sean John from head to toe. I didn't say anything. I noticed and laughed to myself. He was starting to make me believe he needed to be with a sister.

"Did you get Johnson's message?"

"Yeah. We have a 4:00 flight to Norfolk. Are we staying in Virginia Beach?"

"Naw, I lined us up some reservations at the Omni Hotel in Newport News."

"Omni, that's cool. I can do Omni."

I rushed home at lunchtime packed my suitcase and left for the airport about 2:30. Rich and I caught the flight. I realized all of a sudden I hadn't called Geena or Sandy. I decided to use the Airphone. It would sound more legit like it was an emergency. I made my first call. No one answered, so I left a message.

"Sandy, I'm sorry I didn't get a chance to call you back before I left. My job's sending me to Virginia."   I don't have the number, but you can give me a call at the Omni Hotel in Newport News. Talk to ya later."

Now I had to make my second call. I was cool about the second because I knew Geena was at her shop. I dialed the numbers and made the call. The rings sounded like they were going on forever before her answering machine picked up. Ring. Ring. Ring. "Hello." A brother answered the phone. I hung up. I must have dialed the wrong number. Now that I had cleared my head, I called back.

"Hello."

It was the same guy.

"Who is this?"

"Who....is this?" You called here."

"Where's Geena?"

"She ain't here right now. She'll be back soon."

 "Who are you? I asked loudly.

He hung up on me. I played it off like I controlled this situation. I didn't want anybody to know I was hearing dial tone at 30,000 feet. He was disrespecting me by being at my girl's house. If I could get off this plane I would. I sat there seething. Then came those words of support.

"Girl trouble, bro?"

"Naw, I'm good."

"No you aren't. I heard the conversation and so did everybody else on the plane."

"I got to use the bathroom."

"Go ahead and run, but you need to get it out man."

I got up and made my way to the bathroom. I thought Rich was joking, but all passengers were staring at me. They did hear my conversation. Was I talking that loud? When I came out of the lavatory, the flight attendant gave me some water. She said she thought that might cool me down.

We arrived in Norfolk and made our way to the rental car. It was about a thirty-five minute drive to the hotel and Rich was full of conversation.

"I wonder what the women look like in this town."

"Dude, we need to keep our mind focused on the client."

"You need to keep your mind focused on the client."

I got a little irritated by Rich's arrogance, but that was Rich. Then he broke out the good news.

"I already finished the presentation. All you have to do is present it."

"When'd you do it?"

"I had some numbers already on my hard drive. That's what I was working on when you stopped by my cube this morning."

"Cool."

"I got your back. Now tell me about the phone conversation."

I shook my head. "Not right now."

We arrived at the Omni and were greeted by two pleasant front desk clerks, Cindy and Lorranine. It struck me as odd that the sister had a white girl's name, Cindy, and the white girl had a sister's name, Lorraine. Rich was immediately stepping to the plate with Cindy.

"Can I tell you something?" Rich said leaning over the counter in front of Cindy.

"Sure sir." Cindy said still looking down at her computer screen confirming our reservations.

"You have some of the most beautiful eyes."

"Well thank you. Are you flirting with me to get a nicer room?"

"I wasn't flirting at all. You can't embellish the truth."

Cindy smiled blushing.

"Here you are sir. You are in room 913. It's the best room in the house."

"Thank-you . Are you going to join me?"

Cindy starts laughing because she is not sure whether Rich is serious or just flirting.

"No sir. I won't be joining you."

I grabbed Rich before he made a fool of himself.

"Come on man!!!"

As he left he gave Cindy one more parting shot.

"Take care beautiful!!

What I was bewildered about was that Rich had an opportunity to talk to the white girl or the sister and he went out of his way to talk to the sister. I was learning more and more about the human condition of white people. Rich didn't care that the white girl was there. He saw what he believed to be an attractive person and stepped to her. I had just learned another one of life's lessons. If the situation were reversed, I could not have pursued the white girl in front of the sister. But white people see themselves as individuals and don't feel responsible for the actions of other white people. Black people, on the other hand, feel responsible for the actions of other black people. Was that reasonable or were black people putting weight on their shoulders that wasn't realistic? That was my thought for the day.

15

I spent the evening looking at the reports Rich had put together earlier in the day. I modified them a little bit to fit our client, but Rich had done his homework and we were ahead of the curve. I called Rich's room three hours later. There was no answer. Evidently, Rich was on the move and out sightseeing the Hampton Roads area.

I wanted to go out, but my body wasn't feeling up to it. I was still wondering who answered the phone at Geena's house. Now I didn't feel so guilty asking myself the question. Was he the baby's daddy? ...And was Geena taking me for a ride? "Goddamnit, who the hell was that guy?" In my attempt to make some space, I didn't realize Geena had been making her own. The phone call was consuming my left brain and work was consuming my right brain.

I was running some numbers when the phone rang. I'd already talked to Johnson earlier, but I knew he would be calling back to go over my plans for my meeting with the client. So I was expecting his call.

"Hello."

"So, you sneak out of town without seeing anyone?"

"No. Not really."

I couldn't recognize the voice. I had to keep talking, feel them out. I knew it was either Geena or Sandy, but so much was on my mind. I had work, two relationships, Geena's pregnancy, questions on baby-daddy drama. It seemed like the Lord was testing me. Why? Why? Why?

"Girl, you're too much."

"No, I'm not. Do you miss me?

So much was running through my mind, who was this?

"You know I do."

I had to say something to figure out who the hell it was. But what?

"Did you get my call?"

"That's why I'm calling."

"Who was that guy?"

Then all I heard was 'dial tone. Well I guess it wasn't Geena. I messed up. My phone rang back.

"I hate these Sprint phones. My calls are always dropping. I was walking into the hospital. I didn't hear you. What were you saying?"

Good, she didn't hear me. I was able to breath a little. Another call beeped in.

"Hello."

"How's the job coming?"

"Hold on Mr. Johnson, I got somebody on the other line."

I clicked back.

"Sandy?"

"Don't tell me. You have to go? Looks like things are busy here anyway. Call me later."

"I will. Talk to you later."

I hung up from Sandy and returned to Johnson. We went over the meeting, the client profile, and my estimated time of arrival back in Atlanta. He seemed impressed with my progress as a project manager. I was happy with that considering all the baggage I was carrying.

The next morning, I met Rich in the lobby. He looked somewhat drained but pumped.

"I called you. Where were you last night?"

"I didn't do too much. It was Salsa Night at Mitty's, the hotel bar."

"Were the Boriquas looking good?"

"What are Boriquas?"

"It's a term used for Puerto Ricans."

"Yes Sirrrrr!!! Yes Sirrrr!!!! They were lookin' good."

"Man, you ain't right. You ain't right, man."

"You've got women problems as it is. You don't need anything else on your plate."

As much as I didn't want to admit it, Rich was right. On the way to the project we discussed our meetings. What he was responsible for. What I would be responsible for. As we drove down Jefferson Avenue, I thanked him for gathering the information for the morning meetings. He saved us a lot of time. We made a turn onto Mercury Boulevard and we could see the USS Ronald Reagan. It was an aircraft carrier that had been commissioned in honor of the former president. The ship was enormous. It had a huge '76' painted on the side of the island house. I asked Rich if he knew what the 76 stood for. He told me it represented the number in succession of aircraft carriers made. I thought about the enormity of the ship and the amount of dollars being made by the firm. The hair on my arm suddenly stood up. I was suddenly shocked at the amount of responsibility that Johnson had given me. We were set to make millions off this project. I was getting my feet wet in a big way. As we approached the gate, Rich and I tightened our ties and put our game faces on. We were ready to make Smith and Boland a lot of money.

Rich took the front line management. I took the middle managers. Our job was to convince Newport News Shipbuilding that we could increase the revenue take with small changes in their operation. After meeting with the department managers, I slipped in to see how 'White Chocolate' was handling the section managers. When I got there, Rich was putting it down. I was very impressed.

When it was time to work, Rich worked. When it was time to play, Rich played. Hard. Rich had me convinced to take the project and I didn't even work for the shipyard. I took a seat in the back, listened, and on several occasions learned some things. Rich led them exactly where he wanted them to go.

"Tell me Mr. Landrum, what do you think makes a good manager?"

"One who is direct, sets goals, and hits deadlines."

"I agree. What about one who empowers his employees? Allows them to make decisions. When we asked, the first thing the employees said was, the managers don't respect our opinion."

"Not here. We'd be letting the inmates run the asylum."

Rich shook his head in agreement. He was setting Landrum up.

"If you allowed your employees to make some small decisions that affected their job, don't you think they would take more ownership in the tasks they were assigned?"

The room was silent. Landrum didn't want to admit it but he knew Rich had taken him down a path that he had never thought about. The managers began to ask Rich more questions and got more involved in the process. I sat in the back and said nothing. As I enjoyed watching Rich's enthusiasm holding the lecture, I should have paid more attention to coffee mug sitting beside me. I accidentally knocked it in my lap. I spent the remainder of the workshop with Sprite in hand cleaning my pants.

After the workshop, I walked up to congratulate Rich on a great workshop.

"Good class, man."

"Thanks. What happened to your pants? Bathroom is down the hall."

"Funny mofo. Funny. I wasted some coffee on them."

"Oh that was you making all that noise in the back."

Rich broke out in a small chuckle.

"I thought that was one of the clients falling asleep."

"Naw. That was me dropping my mug. I got to go buy some more pants."

"Well, drop me off at the hotel. I'm tired. I didn't get much sleep last night."

I dropped Rich off at the Omni and used the directions that one of my clients gave me to find Patrick Henry Mall. I found a Structure store and went to look for some pants. The two sales associates were nice looking, I really didn't recall which one of them initially helped me. At first, they didn't notice my standing behind them. They were ranting that Michael Vick, the quarterback for the Falcons had just left the store. He left one of the girls a big tip and the other one was trying to help her spend it.

"Excuse me?"

"I'm sorry. Yes, may I help you?"

"I'm looking for the sale pants."

"Okay. They're over here."

I followed the young lady across the room, letting her lead just enough to take a photo examination of her body. The little sister was about twenty-one, but had the body of a twenty-eight year old. We picked out a few pairs of pants. I was going to just purchase a pair, but she convinced me to try them on. I did. We kept talking through the door. Her name was Kelly. I found out she was actually from Detroit and a junior at Hampton University. Hampton was the next city over from Newport News.

"Where do you live in Detroit? Don't tell me. Off Eight Mile Road?"

"I do."

She started laughing.

"Ahhh....So you don't live in Detroit. You live in Southfield."

"You know too much. Nobody knows where Southfield is."

"You don't know nothing 'bout me."

She shouts across the store to her friend.

"He knows where Southfield is."

Her friend walks across the store.

"Is that a city, really?

"Yep. It's a city."

"We thought Kelly was making it up. She got so mad, she stopped saying Southfield and just told everyone she was from Detroit."

Kelly was laughing and excited that someone knew her city.

"So ladies tell me, are there any clubs around here?"

Kelly spoke up.

"It's "Ladies Night" at The Alley.

"The Alley."

"Yeah. It's a club on the corner of Jefferson and Mercury Boulevard."

"It's almost time for me to get off work. Want me to show you?"

I was about to say yeah when I heard a familiar voice behind me. I didn't know anyone in Virginia so I turned slowly. It was Lorraine, the front desk clerk at the Omni."

"I'll show him."

As I turned, I saw her beaming smile.

"How are you?" I said.

"I'm good. Nice ass."

I blushed a little. I looked at my bottom from behind in the display mirror.

"You think?"

The sales girls moved back to the sales register sensing that the situation was a little out of their league.

"Yeah. I'd bite it."

"You are funny."

I noticed that she had several bags and a big ass diamond on her left ring finger.

"Shopping for the husband?"

"No. My sister is getting married and I was picking up

some things for her bridal shower."

"So is the husband invited?"

I was intrigued now. I was deciphering information.

"No husband."

"Big ass ring."

"I'm separated. Have been for the last 10 months."

Now that I had gotten all the information I needed, we could go back to casual conversation.

"So how did you see me?"

"I was walking by the store and who could miss a big 'ol head like that. I started to holler into the store, "Headquarters!!""

Both of us laughed. Then she rescinded.

"I was just joking."

"Oh you are just the regular comedian"

"I am the funniest person you know."

"Right. I'm the funniest person I know."

"Well... a head like that will keep anyone laughing."

I looked over and smiled. She rescinded again.

"Okay. Okay, I'll stop. You wanna go get something to eat? There are a lot of restaurants around here."

"Let's do that. I'm hungry."

I followed Lorraine to Cheer's, a nice little American cuisine restaurant around the corner from the Omni. We actually got a chance to talk. Lorraine told me that she was separated and her husband lived in her house. She lived with her parents. Her father was the owner of a Mercedes Benz dealership in town. I was wondering how a front desk clerk could afford a '99 230 Mercedes.

While sitting at the table, I got an opportunity to study Lorraine's features. She was incredibly tan. She was actually darker than Sandy. Obviously the product of many hours spent in a tanning salon. She had piercing green eyes and fire red hair.

"So, are you Irish?"

"So how many times this week have you eaten collard

greens?"

I choked on my beer.   I knew what was coming next after that statement.

"How stereotypical. I can't believe you."

"I was looking..."

"...At my features and assumed I was Irish. No, I'm not Irish, but you like the way I pushed the collard greens thing in there, didn't you?"

"You are funny."

"I know."

All of a sudden, Lorraine stopped eating. The smile left her face. Her eyes appeared as though they were changing colors in front of my eyes. Her motion stopped. Only her eyes moved as they studied the room. I thought it had dawned on her that she was on an interracial date in the south. We might be in a new a millennium, but the way I saw it the south was still the south.

"Don't move."

I froze.

"Why?"

"My husband just walked in."

I was still frozen.

"What? Are you serious?"

"Yes. I'm serious."

I suddenly realized I had broken rule number 256. Never sit with your back to the door. I had broken one of the most cardinal of rules, and I was about to be punished in a big way. I nonchalantly placed my hands under the table and bald my fists, so I could be prepared if I got stole on. I could see it now. The boss sends me on a thousand mile trip and has to come bail me out of jail. I am so fucked. Out of nowhere, this big Italiano looking guy approached from my backside. He introduced himself.

"How you doing? I'm Chris Tucci."

"How you doing, Chris Tucci." I didn't return my name just in case he wanted to stalk me later.

"What are you up to tonight? I saw your car outside."
He said to Lorraine.

"I was at the mall shopping and decided to grab a bite to
eat."

"Well I'm going to let you guys eat. I'll talk to you
later."

"Okay, we'll talk later."

"You bet we will."

I sat there quiet. I had been bitched out, as Geena
would say. But ready for combat. The conversation lasted
about thirty seconds, but it seemed as if I was sitting in a
lecture that was lasting for hours. I had to sit there and
quantify my thoughts...was I sitting there like a good puppy
or good soldier? Ready for war, swift, silent, and deadly or
waiting to be fed. I didn't know, but I was glad nothing
broke off.

Lorraine focused her attention back to me.

"What?"

She picked up on my evil eye.

"I didn't know he was coming here."

"Sure, you didn't."

"I didn't."

"Okay."

"You look as though you've lost your appetite."

"I have. I'm about go back to the hotel and get me some
sleep."

"Do you know how to get back?"

"Actually, I don't."

"You can follow me. I'll take you back."

I grabbed the check paid for it and we headed to the
parking lot. As I left the restaurant, I had a thought of a
drive-by. Thoughts of the Godfather sitting in bushes,
lying in wait, surveying his victim, surprising his prey rang
in my head. I wasn't even in Los Angeles and my thoughts
were of dying in a drive-by.

"Thanks, for dinner."

"It's the least I could do since my husband interrupted a beautiful dinner."

"Maybe it's for the better, because he definitely wouldn't have liked my next move."

"Make your next move.   Never know what could happen."

I thought about it, hesitated and laughed.

"What are my odds?"

"They look pretty good from here."

"Awww suki suki."

I looked into Lorraine's eyes. There was something missing. She wanted to be held. She wanted to be loved. I wanted to give her that love too, but it would have only been for a couple of hours. I had prided myself on loving pretty women, but I also was a little better than exploiting their vulnerabilities. I kissed Lorraine on the cheek. She smelled good. Another second and her smell would have been intoxicating.

"Thanks for the invitation, but I'm going to pass. I have a long day tomorrow."

"I understand. Follow me. I'll take you back to the hotel."

I followed Lorraine back to the hotel. She did the circular I got you here turn, waved and broke. I waved back and headed into the hotel. I wondered where Lorraine was headed after me. I chalked up one for the brotherhood, cause I knew the Italian Stallion was going to get some "sneak back pooh" that night.

I walked through the lobby and gave Cindy ceremonial wave on my way to my room.

"Hey! Hey!"

"What's up? How was your day?"

"Two people called in sick. We have 100 check-ins, but I can handle it."

"I know you can."

"You have two messages."

"Who from?"

"Don't play me. What'd you do to that girl? She sounded like she was crying. You're a player. Aren't you?"

"Nooooo. Nooooo."

"You ain't got to lie to me, I'm just the girl at the front desk."

"Well...awww."

I looked at Cindy and explored her seriousness and I only picked up nosiness.

"You thought you had me, didn't you? Ha! Ha! I almost fell for it."

"I did have you."

"Close but no cigar."

I grab my messages, waved my hand and headed for the elevator. I looked at the messages in the elevator. One was from Johnson. "How did your meeting go? Give me a call and give me a follow-up." The second one was from Geena. "I deserve a call."

IF IT AIN'T ONE THING
IT'S ANOTHER

16 . . .

*R*ich and I caught a flight back to Atlanta first thing the next morning. After a long couple of days, I called in sick, went home and got some sleep. Just as the saliva started to break the crack in the corner of my mouth, indicating I was sleeping good, the phone rang. My head refused to move from the pillow, but I cracked my eyes enough to stare at the answering machine as it picked up the call.

"Pick up. I know you are there. I called your job and they said you called in sick. Pick Up!"

The euphoria I felt from getting some of the best sleep I've had in a while was gone. I felt like a crack head that looked in his rearview mirror and saw circular blue lights. My high was gone. By the time I decided to pick up the phone, Geena had already left her message, cursed me out, and was gone in a cloud of smoke.

Since I couldn't sleep anymore, I got up and cleaned my house. Picked up my boxer briefs lying on the other side of the bed. I couldn't remember if they were clean or dirty so I did what any red-blooded American brother would do. I gave them the sniff test. I smelled the Downey. I chalked them into my underwear drawer. I vacuumed. Washed some dishes and Armoralled my leather sofa. I was proud. It shined like new money. I pulled open the shades to the sunroom. The light shined in and, combined with the aroma of Lemon Pine Sol, it suddenly seemed as if it were a brand new day. This would be the day that would change my life. I didn't know how. I didn't know when, but somehow this day was different. I poured myself a Courvoisier and Coke, plopped down on my futon, hit the remote and listened to Back in Stride Again by Frankie Beverly and Maze. In that small element of time, I was at peace and everything was good with the world.

The phone rang. I was too far from the caller-Id, figuring it would be Geena or Sandy. I just picked up the phone.

"What's up bruh?!"

It was Vlad. He was on his cellular. He and Marti were rolling down the I-75 freeway headed into downtown Atlanta.

"What's up man?"

"Nothing too much. Cleaning up the crib."

"Me and Marti are headed to the Gourmet Gents thing at the Hilton."

"Is that where the guys cook dishes for the 100 Black Women?"

"Yeah. Why don't you meet us down there?"

"Okay. What time is it being held?"

"From 6 to 9."

"Give me an hour I'll meet you down there."

I hung up from V, jumped in the shower, put on some of my best "smell good", jumped in the truck, and headed downtown.

I got to the Hilton about 7:30. The Hilton was sponsoring several functions so I had to make my way to the concierge to find out where my function was being held.

"Excuse me...Can you tell where the 100 Black Women function is?"

At that moment, I was reminded of the natural maternal instincts of women. There were 3 parties of people asking questions at the same time. The concierge, who was a woman, had taken in, deciphered, and disseminated the inputted data. I thought of my grandmother dealing with her grandchildren. We would be yelling, hollering, and demanding services of her. She could intake all of the information, distinguish our voices, and answer our questions in one fail swoop. I think I was representative of most men, when more than one person at work was talking to me at same time, I had to demand order in the court.

"The Williams party is in the Hanover Ballroom. The Law Conference is in the International Ballroom. ...And the 100 Black women are in the Grand Ballroom."

I followed the directions down both elevators and rode the aroma of good southern cuisine. After I hit the first elevator, I really didn't need any more instructions. All I had to do was follow the beautiful women. They were everywhere, 10's, 9's, and 8's. Most had male escorts. There were a few who came solo, but all were dressed to impress. I walked into the big ballroom and spotted V immediately. He raised his glass and I followed the light shining off the head of the darkest brother in the room. He and Marti were talking to some friends of her's from college. She introduced me to two beautiful women, but I had too much on my plate to process the information.

"What's the word, bruh? I'm glad you came."

"No problem. I needed to get out anyway."

"Marti, you guys are putting on a nice function."

"You know how we do it."

"Yeah, y'all put it down a little bit."

V immediately interrupted.

"What's up with you and Geena?"

"Nothing. Why?"

"Something's up. We saw her at Lenox and she was tripping on your butt."

"What'd she say?"

I know she didn't put my business out in the street.

Geena has gone too far.

"No too much, but her mannerisms told the story. Marti invited her to the wedding."

"You did what?"

"Don't let him lie to you. V invited her. He thought it was funny."

"Why'd you do that? You always got jokes, man."

"I'm sorry, man. We won't send her an invitation, but that shit was kinda funny though."

"Yeah right, you got jokes. Okay, joke man. I'm bringing Sandy, if your shit gets torn up it ain't my fault."

Marti and V made eye contact. "If my wedding gets destroyed, V, I'm holding you responsible." V tried to subdue Marti. "Look baby, she's not coming. I promise."

"Whatever." Marti walked off and began to greet her guests at the Gourmet Gents function.

"Dude, why'd you say that? You big leagued me."

"You started it by inviting Geena to the wedding."

"I was playing."

"You see what happens when you unleash your stupid practical jokes?"

"Whatever. Let's go get something to eat."

V and I walked around the ballroom and tasted all the food. I was suspect of some of the dishes. I knew some of those brothers' wives had fixed those dishes for them. One brother fixed grits with a ladle mix of cheese and shrimp. I looked at the brother and knew he didn't prepare that dish. It either came from a woman or culinary expertise. He worked at City Hall. Case solved. I wanted to find his wife so I could get the recipe.

V and I held the room hostage as we attempted to taste every dish in the room. As we tasted a piece of cheesecake, I touched V because this brother looked familiar.

"You know him?"

"That's Franklin Pope."

"That ain't Franklin Pope."

"I'm telling you, that's Franklin Pope. Watch this. Franklin."

The brother turned around. It was Franklin plus 130 pounds.

"What's happening fellas?"

"Not too much."

Franklin was running for City Council. I looked around and was amazed. I thought of my grandmother talking about 'grown folks.' She would often tell Kareem and I to stay out of grown folks business. Now we were 'grown folks.' We were getting married, having babies, running for city council. Not necessarily in that order. Franklin and V reminisced about 'playing the dozens' against each other in Mays High's cafeteria. As more people started to converge on what had been reported as the best cheesecake in the room, V and I decided to exit stage left. However, Franklin would not let us leave until we promised he had our vote. Both of us agreed, even though neither one of us lived in the city of Atlanta anymore. We figured we'd probably volunteer and work on his campaign.

V noticed Marti cleaning off tables, noting it was time to go home so he decided to help her. We parted ways and I followed the crowd and headed to my car. Once in my car, I didn't want to drive all the way back to College Park, so I decided to go over to Geena's house since we needed to talk anyway. I tried to call before I got there but the calls kept going straight to her answering machine. It didn't matter, I knew she'd wake up. At least to curse me out.

After eating all that food, I felt fat, dumb, happy, and not to mention sleepy again. I slipped my key into the lock, slowly turned the key and moved into the house. I was as quiet as a cat. I stopped by the kitchen to get some water, which I wolfed down quickly.

I unbuttoned my shirt as I walked down the hall. As I approached the door, I was juiced up and ready to slip in next to Geena's warm body. At that moment, I imagined opening the door and seeing two bodies lying in Geena's bed. I would count them again. "1, 2." The wind had left my body. Geena was sleep, butt-naked in the bed with another man.

I am really confused, because not only was the brother sleeping on my side. He is sleeping there as if it were his side. I make my way and sit down in the lounger next to Geena's side of the bed. Geena must have feel my presence because she cracks her eyes looks me in the face and turns over. There is a delay in the processing. After about five seconds her mind has processed the fact I am in the room as well. There was quick roll back this time to see if she is imagining my face.

I blinked back to reality, took my hand off the doorknob and left Geena's house. My imagination was running wild and I could not be responsible for my actions in the event that art imitated life.

I jumped in the truck and drug my ass back to College Park. I arrived at my house, sleepy and delirious I wandered into the bedroom and slimed into bed. As I rolled to the middle of the bed it smelled sweet. It was the smell of Warm Vanilla Sugar. I jumped up. Geena was in my bed. I jumped out of bed and cut on my floor based halogen lamp.

"Are you surprised to see me?"

"Ah...No. What's up baby? I just came from your house."

"Really? So you just popped up over my house without calling?"

"What's wrong with that? You popped over mine."

"Anyway, why haven't you returned my phone calls?"

"I did call you."

"When did you call me?"

"Last Tuesday, before I left for Hampton Roads."

"Right. I didn't get any messages from you."

I leaned over the bed and passionately kissed Geena on the forehead.

"Ask the brother who answered the phone, he can confirm my call."

"Huh?"

"I said, ask the brother who answered the phone. He got my message."

"Ummm. I left the iron on at my house."

Geena jumped up and grabbed her jeans like an iguana that had just spotted a cricket.

"Geena, who was the guy?"

"I don't know what you're talking about?"

"There was a guy who answered your phone when I called."

"I let Jordan sleep over one night. I left early the next morning. She had better not have invited anybody over."

Jordan was Geena's childhood friend from the East Lake Meadow Projects. They had been friends for twenty years.

"Are you serious? Let me put my stupid face on and you tell me again, I might fall for that the second time around."

"Why would I lie to you?"

"I don't know. That's what I'm trying to figure out."

I tried to look in Geena's eyes to find some semblance of truth. There was none. Right then, right there, Geena was void of the very two things I'd come to cherish. Her trust and honesty.   During our argument, I had blocked the bedroom door to prevent her from leaving. I was prepared to physically restrain her to get some closure, but I had also learned another lesson from my grandfather. Never cross a desperate woman, and as tired as I was, jail was not on my mind tonight.

Without any words, Geena broke free of my grip and rushed out the door. Before I could get to the sunroom, she had gotten in the car, started it, and the only evidence of her presence was the sight of her taillights leaving my complex.

I took a shower and laid down, but I couldn't sleep. Visions of Geena danced in my head. Was she lying? Was I even the father of her baby? My innocence soon turned to anger when I started to think of Geena pinning a baby on me that wasn't even mine. How could she?

My adrenaline was flowing so strong, I got up and fixed myself a bowl of Raisin Bran and watched some cable, Skinemax, which was going full speed. With all that was going on in my life, sex was the last thing on my mind. I decided to watch World News Latenight. I figured I would scope the globe to see what I had to be grateful for and that I had no real problems. Alison Stewart assured me that there were no controversies going on in the world but mine. Thank you, Alison.

I fell asleep on the sofa around 4 a.m. My alarm clock screamed at me about 6:30. I stumbled to my feet cursing the world, even in the shower sleep refused to leave my body. I managed to stay on schedule and catch my 7:38 train. I wobbled into work. No good mornings for anyone.

"What's up with you today?"

I looked up... it was Mike. He looked as though he was refreshed and ready to conquer the world.

"I don't even want to talk about it."

"Come on. You can tell your boy. What's up? Talk to me. That's what I pay ya fo."

We laughed.

"You are too much, man."

"I heard we got the Newport News account. Congratulations."

"We got it?"

"Hell yeah, boy! You should have seen Rich and I. We put it down. Rich put some figures for Saving Evaluation that definitely sold the project."

At that point, Rich came around the corner. "Congrats man. Did you hear?"

"I just heard. You did a good job. I won't forget it."

"I want to stay on this team."

Mike and I both shouted, "Don't worry. You ain't going anywhere."

"Okay, remember what you said. I got to go do some work."

Mike followed Rich.

"Yeah. Me too."

They went back to their cubicles. The good news had awakened me and I was working on a natural high. I had been emailed a list of possible future accounts. I highlighted the ones that I could possibly take on and hoped Johnson would assign one of them to me. The phone suddenly rang. When I answered, either I was still on a natural high or I could feel Sandy on the other end of the phone.

"Hello."

"Hey baby."

"What's happening beautiful?"

"How was your trip? Did you miss me?"

"I did. Were you feeling that all the way back in Atlanta?"

"I thought I was feeling a little tingle, but didn't know what it was." Sandy laughed. " I know I didn't call you but I knew it was the first project you would be in charge of so I wanted to let you work."

"Guess what?"

"What?"

"We got it."

"Congratulations! We have to go celebrate."

"Yes we do. Why don't you call V and Marti so all of us can go out?"

"Okay, I'll do that."

"I have a surprise for you too."

"What is it?"

"I'll tell you tonight. I have to go. I'll talk to you later."

"Okay baby."

Sandy hung up. I looked at the phone and smiled. I felt warm and fuzzy on the inside. It was something about getting Sandy's satisfaction that made me feel complete. It was like she was my other half.   I daydreamed about why Sandy made me feel complete and in the eight years Geena and I had dated, I never felt that with her.

I paged V and told him to grab Marti and let's meet at Spondivit's.   I told him I was bringing Sandy.   Both of us wanted to share our good news with them.   We decided to meet about 7:30.   After work, Sandy picked me up in front of my building.   I could tell she was excited.   Her eyes sparkled.   I couldn't wait to hear her news.

"I'm scared to get in the car.."

"Why?" She said smiling from ear to ear.

"You are so excited, looks like you are about to shoot firecrackers from your ass."

She laughed, "Shut up stupid.   You are so silly."

"What happened?   Why are you so excited?"

"I'll tell you at dinner."

"Tell me now."

"No, I'll tell you at dinner in front of everybody."

"Why? I'm your boyfriend."

"...And my boyfriend will find out at dinner."

I knew it had to be important.   The ants wouldn't stay still in her pants.   Then I thought, what if Sandy said she was pregnant.   The wind suddenly released from my sails. That would be all I needed right now.   Two women pregnant at the same time, Lord knows I didn't need that.   As we got closer to the restaurant, I became quiet and more reclusive. Sandy was driving and dancing to R. Kelly's new jam.   At first she was into the song, then she noticed I wasn't participating.

"What's wrong?   You haven't said anything in five minutes."

"Nothing's wrong.   Why do you ask?"

"R. Kelly is your favorite and you didn't hum a word."

"I don't like that song."

"Yeah right. You like everything R. Kelly makes."

Before I could justify my behavior, a ghettofied Sedan de

Ville cut us off forcing Sandy to almost hit the center median. Angry at the world, I shouted out of the car.

"What the fuck are you doing??!!! You need to look where you're going! Punk motherfuckas."

"Goodness, I've never heard you curse like that."

"They're trying to kill somebody."

"Hell. You keep shouting out the car like that, we'll get killed for real."

"Whatever. I'll die for this."

"Okay, Billy Blanks. You're gonna kill'em with Tae-Bo?"

"You are just the comedian. Aren't you? Get off at the next exit."

Sandy cut over two lanes and exited the freeway. We pulled into Spondivit's parking lot, I was still seething about almost getting killed. As we walked up the hill to the restaurant, Sandy was cracking jokes.

"Stop. Relax. Release. Stop. Relax. Release."

"Ha Ha Ha. I told you that you need to take that act on the road."

"You know I'm funny."

"You are not funny."

We made eye contact and I began to smile. Sandy caught me smiling immediately.

"Aah!!! You want to laugh. Let it out."

"Our company is here already."

"Where?"

"That's V's Jag right there."

"When did V get a Jag?"

"About 2 months ago. You know him. Always flossing."

"You too."

"Please."

"What? You've had 3 cars since we've known each other. That was 2 and half years ago."

"Whatever."

"You don't need to go to the dentist this year."

"What does that mean?"

"All you do is floss."

We both started laughing as we walked into the restaurant. The doorman picked up on our joy as we cracked the door.

"Can I hang out with y'all?"

Sandy responded laughing, "Sure, the world can hang out with us."

"Can I have a little of what you guys are having too."

I helped him out, "We're high on life, bruh."

"Ya'll must be celebrating."

"Yeah, how'd you know?"

"Too much positive energy."

"We were supposed to be meeting another couple here."

"Oh yeah, they're on the patio. The other couple high on life."

"That would be them."

"Follow me. They're in the sunroom."

We followed Sammy the doorman into the sunroom and there sat V and Marti. I couldn't believe it, they were already eating. Marti was excited when she saw Sandy.

"What's up, girl?!"

"Too much. Too much. How are the wedding plans?"

"Busy. Still looking for a dress. But I think we're going on a Med cruise for the honeymoon. We've been talking about Monaco, Istanbul, and Morocco."

"That's sounds too good. Can I go?"

"Come on girl."

"Ya'll can pack me in a suitcase."

At the same time, I was talking to V.

"What ya'll doing?

"What?"

"Why are you guys eating?"

"We're not eating."

"What's that?"

"Mushroom stuffed crab."

"....And?"

"Shut your cakehole. It's just appetizers. Have one."

"Shut up."

"Okay."

V stopped talking and picked up another mushroom and ate it in front of me. "This is too good." V gestured to our waitress to come over. This fine little young sister strolled over. I could tell V had been flirting with her or she saw him drive up in the X-Type.

Even with Atlanta being the epicenter of the new black renaissance, it had been a long running joke that Atlanta brothers bought into it hook, line, and sinker. If they made fifty thousand, they'd spend forty-eight showing everybody they made fifty. We owned Beamers, Benzs, Acuras, Jags, and Lexuses and still lived with our mamas. We had come to believe success was ninety percent perception. The motto of Atlanta brothers was "Fake it 'til you make it."

"Yes sir. Are you guys ready to order?"

"Well I was just going to order the drinks, but how about we get 2 buckets of crab legs and some lobster tails."

Everybody chimed in.

"Sounds good to me."

"Okay beautiful, that's our order. Oh yeah and a couple cosmopolitans for the ladies and Jack and cokes for the fellas." Marti interrupted V.

"Vlad, excuse me?"

"Oh, baby I forgot. She'll just have a Sprite."

As the waitress left, Marti gave V a sharp elbow to the ribs.

"What do you mean, okay beautiful?"

"Ouch! It's just a figure of speech."

"Not in this relationship, it isn't."

"Baby, it was just a figure of speech. I look at you and know. Right here, right now....being here with you is urgent than a motherfucka."

The table went silent.

"Shut up. You are so full of shit." Marti snickered.

We all burst out laughing at V's unoriginal ass. Marti made eye contact with Sandy and gestured.

"Huh, so that's my prize? Lucky me."

The girls laughed and high fived each other. V responded quickly.

"Oh so everybody got jokes."

Our food came and we ate, laughed, got liquored up, ate, and laughed some more. V kills me. Whenever there's company, V tells the story of how everyday after school I would drive by the school in my '74 Dodge with the windows rolled up, bumping my music. My head would be just rocking back and forth. But there was just one catch, my car didn't have a radio, nor did it have air conditioning. So I would be in the car burning up and rocking my head to air. Looking back I had to admit, it was the beginning of the floss. One day, there was a huge traffic jam coming out of the parking lot at my school and I was in my usual routine, window rolled up, and I passed out from dehydration. It was 110° in the car and all I could remember was stuff getting a little blurry until everything went black. The next thing I knew the paramedics had me stretched out on the ground. Everybody at school found out I'd been perpetrating air and a sound system. I was ribbed on everyday until I graduated. College has long been the perfect opportunity for someone to reinvent themselves. Perfect their imperfections, but V went to college with me so my story followed and had remained alive for the last 15 years.

V found every occasion to be the perfect opportunity to tell that story and today was no different. After it was over, Sandy made eye contact with Marti, then looked me in the eye.

"So, you're my prize?"

The girls laughed and stomped their feet and high fived each other. I personally didn't find the humor. All of them knew I was the funniest person at the table, but didn't want to admit it. V came to my rescue and broke up the laughter.

"So we're here and still don't know what we're celebrating. Why are we here bruh?"

"I sold a five million dollar account for the firm."

V shouted with excitement for me.

"Damn! My boy! My boy! We're rich. How much of that do you get? I need to borrow five dollars."

"Yeah right...a small bonus at the end of the project."

"That's all? Bruh, they don't appreciate you. You need to be out."

"I'm comfortable. I need to get to the next level to get the real bucks. But they're grooming me for that."

V responded defensively, "Hell, it better be something in it for us.

"Us?! Where did we get us?

"Shudde!!! Nigga. It's just like we've been married. I deserve something. I've been listening to you bitch for twenty years."

"Shut up. You're stupid."

"I'm still your boy though. Let's toast my man's big account."

We all raised our glasses.

"To my boy and hoping that the company who's pimping him now, gets him to the next level.   TO PIMPING!"

V, Marti, Sandy, and I tapped our glasses.

"TO PIMPING!"

I had forgotten Sandy was celebrating too and I didn't know what it was.

"Wait! Wait, everybody! My baby has something to celebrate as well. Go ahead baby. Tell us."

Sandy's smile moved from joyous to hesitant. She seemed to want us to know but not right now. Marti supported me.

"Tell us Sandy. What do you have going?"

I thought to myself. Please don't let her say she's

pregnant.

"Well.....I been accepted to a trauma program at NYU Downtown Hospital in Manhattan.   It's the best in the country."

After blurting out her acceptance to the program, Sandy stared at us for approval.   V, always being 50 percent antagonist, 50 percent mediator, and seeing my reaction he decided to promote the latter.

"That's good, doc! We are just making money all over the place."

Marti followed her man.   Congratulations Sandy! When does the program start?

"In 45 days."

I jumped in immediately, "You're going to New York in 45 days! What about me?"

"This is about my professional growth, baby."

"But what about me?!"

"Well, do you want to move up with me?"

"No! I don't want you to take it!"

Just then Sammy the doorman came over to quiet the set.

"Hey, you guys are a little loud. Can you quiet it down just a little?"

V gestured to Sammy with a nod. I stared into space. I thought the relationship was just starting to get somewhere and now she was leaving. What was that about?   It just didn't click.   Somehow I knew if she left Atlanta, things would never be the same. I snatched my coat away from the table and stormed out of the restaurant. As I left the restaurant, I heard V say, "Stay here. I got him."

I rushed into the parking lot looking for my truck. I needed to ride. I needed some air. Looking around in circles, I suddenly realized that I hadn't driven. V came running out behind me.

"Hey, Man! What was that about?"

"She is just going to disregard this relationship. What

the fuck is that about?"

"Dude, this isn't about you. This is about her career."

"What about me?"

"What about you? Can I ask you a question?"

"What?"

"Why are you being so selfish?"

"Selfish? Selfish? This is coming from the brother who strung Marti along for five years. What a hypocrite!"

"We aren't talking about me. We are talking about you. Besides, I didn't force Marti to stay. She stayed because she wanted to. You are trying to force this woman to stay because of your own self-interests. I thought you were better than that."

"I am."

"Well, why don't you act like it?"

"I don't want to. Damn it, I love her man! ...I love her."

At that moment, V stopped being aggressive and sat on the wall next to me. He put his arm on my shoulder.

"I know bruh. I know. I see the way you look at her. She's special. Why do you think I didn't fuck her?"

Just then I remembered how V could make a bad situation funny. I smiled. V looked me with a serious look.

"Who said something funny?"

"Dude...you're stupid."

We both laughed out loud.

"Where would you be without me?" V said smiling. "Dog, let her go. If it's meant to be she'll come back."

"That's what I'm afraid of. She ain't coming back."

"She'll be back. Let's go back inside. Besides you haven't heard the real bad news."

"What real bad news?"

"About your Falcons."

"What about the Falcons?"

"They traded Kevin Trotter to the New York Giants."

"What?"

"Yep, today about five o'clock. I meant to tell you when you came in."

"He was the best player on the team. They traded Trotter."

Trotter was my man. My savior on Sundays in the fall. My football messiah. The Falcons lone bright spot. My man Kevin Trotter was gone. I paused for a second. Kevin ......Trotter. It hit me. I knew the guy with Sandy at the Boney James concert looked familiar. Kevin was Kevin Trotter. Wait a second, Kevin Trotter gets traded to New York. Sandy accepts a position at a New York hospital. What a coincidence or was it? I felt like I had gotten the long invisible shaft. I didn't mention my suspicions to V. We strolled back into the restaurant.

"What's up? We're back." V said.

"I want to apologize to you guys. I was being an ass-o-holic."

Sandy stood up and hugged me.

"I'm sorry baby, but I really just made the decision today."

"I know you did."

"You did? How'd you know?"

"Hmmm.....I figured you would have told me before now if you hadn't."

"You know I would have. The letter had been sitting on my desk for weeks. It was coming down to the deadline and I had to make a decision."

"...and it came today."

"Today was the day."

I looked in Sandy's eyes and wanted to believe her. Desperate to believe her but it never came. She hadn't been honest with me. I could feel the dishonesty in the air. Marti and V asked the waitress for a to-go box, signaling it was time to go. Sandy kissed me on the cheek, her way of putting up a white flag. I took her white flag and raised a red one. But that was for me to know and her to find out.

"Baby, you ready to go? These guys are taking food with them."

V cut into our conversation, "I'm not wasting anything. My food is going with me. Y'all want any of these oysters?" V looked over Marti, "Baby, we're taking the oysters home."

"I don't need any oysters to look through bridal magazines."

I asked Sandy if she wanted to take anything home. She agreed to let Marti and V have the extra food. Well, let V have the extras. We split the check, group hugged, and said our good-byes.

"Excuse me Ms.? Can I get a ride home?"

"I don't know. Maybe...If?"

"What would that if be?"

"If you are sponsoring a sleepover. I may be too tired and too horny to go home."

"That definitely can be arranged."

"Well sir, I think we've entered into a verbal agreement."

I put my arm around Sandy and she put her arm around my waist as we headed for the car. We passed another couple on their way to dinner. We heard the woman say, "They make a beautiful couple." Sandy and I made eye contact and smiled. Her green eyes pierced my soul and I knew I had to distance myself from this woman. I had to detach myself emotionally if I was going to play the game.

Sandy and I arrived at my apartment. I walked in and instantly began to check my mail. Sandy walked into the bedroom. After checking my mail, I began to check phone messages. When I got to the third message, I felt two arms wrapping around me and hardened nipples poking the small of my back. It instantly rose my manhood. Even though Sandy's embrace was warm and inviting, there was something different about her embrace this time. Sandy didn't make it known, but it felt like a good-bye embrace. As if her body was letting me know this was the last time we would make love. I turned around and looked in her eyes.

My eyes slowly inspected the beautiful copper tone of
Sandy's naked body, her beautiful toes. Her ass formed the
mold for the letter "P". I aggressively grabbed the back of
her hair and pulled her head back and began to kiss her
neck. Sandy moaned with ecstasy. Right here. Right now, I
was doing my job. I kneeled in front of Sandy and began
kissing her hips, running my tongue around her navel. I
started from her navel and ran my tongue down her thighs
to her knees. I stopped in between to smell her treasure. It
was mixture of Plumeria and work day. Sandy giggled, but
she never asked me to stop.

I stood up grabbed her naked hips and raised her on to
the day bar. I started at her chest and slowly moved down
burying my head between her thighs. Kissing and sucking.
Sucking and kissing. If it was going to be my last time, I
was going to give her all she wanted.

Sandy wasn't backing down. She invited everything I
was willing to give her and asked for a little more. She
rested back on her elbows to look at me love her face to face.
Eye to eye. Sandy reached over and grabbed the bottle of
Sue Bee Honey sitting on the counter and began to pour the
honey from the crest of her Y chromosome up to her
nipples. And suddenly, I had been tasked with removing the
sugar soaked syrup from her sweet smelling body. I would
have made any grizzly proud.

Thirty minutes after we began, we both knew what we
were doing needed to finished in my bedroom. I picked
Sandy up Officer and a Gentleman style and walked her into
my bedroom. I laid her down on my bed. The only
illumination that exposed her body was the glow from the
streetlight between the blinds of my bedroom. As our
bodies met as one, I was determined to show my back was
strong enough that two hundred years ago I would have
been considered a buck. As pleasure filled Sandy's eyes the
thought of her leaving me consumed my mind. The thought
of her leaving me to be with another man began to enrage

me.

"Who's is it?"

"Your's baby."

"Tell me again. Who's pussy is this!"

"Your's! It's yours!"

I dug in like I was entrenched and focused. I went harder and harder. What started out as pleasure suddenly became painful. Physically and psychologically. Sandy jumped from under me and escaped to the other side of the bed.

"What the hell are you doing?! Bastard! That hurt."

"What?! We were making love."

"That wasn't love. That was hate."

Sandy began to gather her clothes. As she put on her panties, she mumbled to herself. Words that I couldn't make out, but I somehow deducted that they were unpleasant.

She walked out leather coat and shoes in hand. As she stormed through the living room she shouted, "Call me when you learn how to treat somebody! Bastard!" I heard the door slam.

I sat there with a half-baked smile on my face. What started out as a perverted sense of self-satisfaction quickly became a frown. I was ashamed at what I had done. I had hurt someone I cared for deeply. I wasn't proud of that. I didn't have the balls to call her, but I hoped she'd call me when she got home. I sat there and waited. No call. I dozed off but was awakened when the phone rang at 2 a.m. I answered the phone groggy.

"Hello...hello. Baby, I'm sorry."

"GG died!"

"Huh?"

"GG died."

It was my mother telling me that my grandmother had passed.

17 . . .

I only got small pockets of sleep the rest of the night. All I could think about was GG with sprinkles of Sandy in between. My grandmother had passed. The feeling in my stomach was this could not be true. Not GG. I pleaded with God not to let this be true. I had convinced myself that this had to be a dream. GG was suppose to live forever. During those pockets I replayed many of the things that GG and I had done in my years growing up. I awoke, called my job, packed some clothes, and met my parents at their house. I rode with them to my grandmother's house in Alabama.

The ride down Interstate 20 was the longest, quietest ride of my life. Not one of us spoke as much as twenty words. My mother stared out of the passenger window. I peeked at her reflection against the window. She was blank. Her mother was gone. When my mother hurt, I hurt.

Her pain swallowed the car and there was nothing that my father and I could do. My grandmother's strength had been such an influence in mother's life. I used to watch my mother's siblings imitate her and compare her to GG. She was always defiant, saying she would never act like GG. She was her own woman. Twenty years later, it was hard to distinguish between the two. When she did speak she spoke as though GG was still living.

"I wonder if I should have brought her Christmas present."

My father jumped in.

"If you forgot it, that's okay."

It seemed as though we got to Birmingham very quickly, but stretching the next 90 miles to Livingston seemed like an eternity. Livingston was a small town in southwestern Alabama where at one time black folks were supposed to know their place. Now their mayor was black.

My mother called Kareem. He was catching the first flight east. She wanted me to drive back to Birmingham to pick him up. I figured I would enlist my cousin Tre, to ride with me. As we got off the freeway it sunk in, we were going to my grandmother's house and she wasn't going to be there. My heart felt heavy but I knew I had to be strong for my mother. While I was growing up, I viewed Livingston as a place to mess with cows, chase horses, and breath the way no one on earth did. It was the country. Not the way people along the upper-east coast and the west coast consider Southern people country. It was the country. Rural. That was the way of life. As much as I liked going there, I hated helping my grandmother shell peas. We had done that twice a week in the summer. But Livingston was a hibernation zone because there was no way my friends in Atlanta could ever know I was sitting around shelling peas. It was many years before I realized there is dignity in all honest labor.

It wasn't my father that got me into sports. It was my grandmother. She bought me my first baseball glove. She loved the Braves. Back then TV didn't come in so well in the country at night so she had them locked into the transistor radio. She would throw the baseball and I'd catch it. My father drove 370 miles roundtrip to pick-up GG, and bring her to my first little league game. I refused to go in until GG got there. I wanted to show her that her hard work had paid off. GG was more than a grandmother, she was my protector, my savior, my friend.

When I was 8 years old, I can't remember what I had done, but D gave me the worst whipping that I had ever had.   I called my grandmother to tell on him.   She convinced my parents to let Kareem and I come to Livingston for the summer.   That summer I was willing to make the switch off, shelling peas.   When Kareem and I got off the Greyhound, she said to me, "Baby, you ain't got to worry 'bout whippings no more this summer." Accompanying that statement was a big hug and kiss.   My grandfather worked at a textile mill.   He was around only a few hours a day, enough for Kareem to get his daily knee-pony rides.

My grandfather died when I was 10.   I had never seen GG so depressed.   But she never cried.   Sometime during the After-Service Dinner she managed to break loose to come check on Kareem and I who were in the back bedroom playing.   After 3 games of Uno, we began to see a flow of tears stream down GG's face.   Kareem who was 6 at the time stood up, walked over to GG rubbing her tears away with his small hands.

"GG, I'll never leave you. We will be with you forever."

GG gave Kareem and I a big hug.   There was so much love in that day.   You could have filled the Superdome.   As much life as GG had, a little of it was stolen from her that day.

From time to time, GG would cook dinner and set an extra plate for Pa Pa, then she would realize Pa Pa wasn't there anymore.   I became really angry with religion during that time, because I couldn't figure out why God would leave GG alone.

Kareem and I sat on her floor one summer day playing Monopoly.   She was sitting in her chair monitoring my innate ability to cheat my little brother out of his money.   Out of nowhere I began to quiz my grandmother about religion.

"GG, do you believe in God?"

"Yes, baby why do you ask? We go to church on Sundays. Don't we?"

"Yes ma'am. But I don't believe in God."

Kareem grabbed his baseball glove and headed for the door.

"I'm going outside. Lightning 'bout to strike in here."

He was gone before either one of us could get the next word out. She asked me again.

"Why would you say that?"

"Because he took Pa Pa from us. ...And now you're alone when we leave. If God existed he wouldn't do that."

My grandmother sat me down that day and told me that everything happened for a reason. She wasn't mad at God and neither should I. She taught me that God has a plan and sometimes God's plans don't coincide with ours. In a matter of seconds, she brought me back to Jesus. 'Cause I knew GG wouldn't lie to me.

My parents and I arrived at my grandmother's house late in the afternoon. We walked through the door. There were people everywhere. Most were church members from GG's church. My aunt and uncle met my mother at the door. The veins in their eyeballs dominated their faces. They'd pulled out old photo albums and reflected on their childhood growing pains. They had laughed and cried, shared stories, denied rumors and blamed the most embarrassing moments on relatives who were not there to defend themselves. I immediately searched the room for a familiar face. I spotted Tre, who was in the kitchen fixing a church sponsored meal. I hugged my aunt, uncle and moved past church folk, distant cousins, and family friends to get to the kitchen. Tre and I made eye contact. His eyes were red as well.

"You alright brother?"

"Yeah man, I'll make it. All cried out."

"Yeah. I had some cries on my way down."

I looked around to see if anything was out of place.

"Everything looks the same."

"Yeah. You know she wanted to keep everything the same as if Pa Pa was still here."

Tre broke down and started crying again. He rested his head on my shoulder. I patted his back to console him, but my aunt quickly ran into the kitchen to console Tre.

I sat down next to my mother and father as if I were nine again as they reacquainted themselves with relatives. Everyone wanted to know where Kareem was. My mother repeated herself what seemed like a hundred times that Kareem was flying into Birmingham and would be in about 10. When I got a chance, I asked Tre to ride with me to Birmingham. It would be a chance for him to get out of the house. He agreed.

Our ride to Birmingham was quiet at first. I broke the silence with a joke.

"What do you say to a woman with two black eyes?"

"I don't know? What?"

Tre' never made eye contact. He answered continuing his blank stare out the window.

"Nothing. You already told her twice."

I heard Tre' snicker. The snicker burst out into a small laugh.

"You need to be doing Stand-Up."

"I know. I've been trying to tell people I'm funny. They don't want to listen."

Tre' cleared his throat, his mind was off the events of the day for a second.

"So how are things in Atlanta?"

"They are good. Trying to make ends meet."

"Yeah, okay."

"How are things in Dallas?"

"They're cool. I just moved from Oakcliffe."

"Where'd you move?"

"I moved a little further south. A little spot called De Soto."

"Yeah. One of my friends on the Cowboys lives there."
"Yeah a couple of the Cowboys live in De Soto."
"You're putting it down like that."
"Not really. Just trying to do my thing."
"When you going to get married?"
"I was waiting on you. I wanted to be your best man."
"Keep waiting."
"I know that's right. My girl came down with me."
"Really which one was she?"
"She was the one in the kitchen wearing the green shirt."
"She is tight bruh. You did a good job."
"She's okay. Bugs the shit out of me sometimes."
"I feel you. Mine too."
"Where is your girl?"
"She didn't come. She's on punishment."
"I feel you, man. They will act up sometimes."
Tre and I understood each other. There was no
generation gap between us. I was the oldest grandson by 15
months. He was second. Tre' followed me to college at
Clark Atlanta. He went to the American High School in
Germany where my aunt was in the Army. After graduation,
I got a job. Tre' went on to grad school and got his MBA.
He got a job at a public relations firm in Dallas and had
been there ever since.
We got to the airport a little before 11. Kareem was
already at baggage claim. I could tell he was tired and
distraught.
"Where the hell have y'all been?"
"That's how long it took."
"Why didn't you leave earlier? What's up Tre'?
Tre' reached his hand over the seat to welcome Kareem.
"Kareem."
"How's everybody doing?"
"All cried out."
"Well I got some more cries to give. How's mom?"
"She's holding up. But she's gonna break any minute if

she hasn't already."

The car was quiet on the way back to Livingston. We had a choice of two CDs. We had DMX and Ron Isley and neither seem appropriate. So we elected to ride back in silence. When we got off the highway, I could feel the three of us beginning to choke up. As the car traveled down the dark winding country we saw no lights. Kareem mentioned that Livingston would not be confused with LA, Atlanta, or Dallas. Livingston reminded us of the Life movie with Eddie Murphy and Martin Lawrence. They had everything from cows to outhouses. I always recalled my grandmother having a bathroom, but legend has it she got hers just before I was born.

When we got to the house, Kareem ran in to look for my mother. Kareem hadn't seen my parents since last Thanksgiving. He got in the house, scanned the room for my grandmother. Hoping that this was all a sick joke. When my mother revealed herself amongst all the people who were in the house, her expression told the story. He instantly began to cry. I saw them embracing as I entered the house. A tear ran down my face. I had to hold it. I had to be strong for my family.

The family talked well into the night over the next several days. We would wake up each morning looking like death warmed over. On the day of the funeral, the house turned into what seemed like the "Brady House" with so many people moving to get dressed at the same time. There was only one bathroom and fifteen people had to fit. Everybody finished just under the wire, in time for the limousines to arrive.

At the funeral, the choir sang everything from the old Negro spirituals to Jesus is Love by the Commodores. I heard stories about my grandmother I had never heard before. Stories about her antics as a child, stories about her as a teenager, stories about her in the civil rights movement. My grandmother in the civil rights movement, I was dumbfounded at what a proud woman she had been. She and Pa Pa had been the Matriarch and Patriarch of the community and a thousand people were coming to pay their respects. I had been okay throughout the ceremony, but as they began to lower GG into the ground I found myself breaking down. My eyes were watering and my shoulders were trembling. I began to cry like a baby. I felt someone come up to console me, I rested my head on her shoulder. When she passed me a handkerchief to wipe my face, I looked up. It was Geena. What was Geena doing here? How did she know? Geena had driven almost 400 miles to come to my grandmother's funeral. Geena escorted me as we walked away from the gravesite.

"What are you doing here?"

"She was my GG too."

My grandmother had a way of treating everyone special and making everyone feel wanted. I stopped just before I got into the limo and turned to look back at GG's casket.

"I love you GG."

Geena and I walked around as a couple without any problems. In fact, a few people asked us how long we had been married. Before I could speak up. Geena answered and said we were working on it.

18 . . .

My parents stayed behind in Livingston to settle GG's estate. I rode back to Atlanta with Geena. We dropped Kareem off at the airport. Kareem made a comment that he liked Geena's extra weight. I didn't entertain the comment. I moved on to the next topic. But I thought to myself, "Brother, you have no idea." Geena and I made small talk until we got to the Georgia border. I decided to speak up.

"How have you been?"

"Morning sickness is killing me."

"So, have you decided what you're gonna do?"

"No I haven't. Have you decided what you want me to do?"

That was a double edge sword that I wasn't prepared to touch 100 miles from home without my car. I knew I had to walk a tight rope. Geena's attitude could blaze as red as the leaves we passed on the highway against the fall landscape.

"Geena...who was the guy who answered the phone."

"Joey."

"Who the fuck's Joey?"

"Why are you cussing at me?!"

"Why are you playing games with me?!"

"Well you don't have to be cussing at me."

"Stop avoiding the question!"

"Okay. Okay."

"He's a guy that's been pursuing me."

"You let him answer your phone. What the fuck was that about?"

"Stop cussing at me! I didn't know he answered the phone."

"Where were you? You left him in your house?"

"Hold on! Hold up...Slow...your roll. Is it your house? I wanted it to be your house but you...didn't want it to be your house."

She did have a point, but I wasn't willing to concede in the heat of the battle.

"How long has this guy been around?"

Geena hesitated as if she was concentrating on the road. Looking at the road. Looking in her rearview. Never looking at me.

"How...long....has....this..."

"A year."

"A year! A year, Geena?! You know what? I'm through with it!"

I shook my head in disgust. It would be another 15 minutes before one of us spoke another word. During the break in excitement I thought to myself, how could Geena do this to me? Two-timer. When a flash of Sandy crossed my mind. I felt so small in my attempt to belittle her. What I had accused her of doing I had done for the last two years.

"Did you ever sleep with him?"

"Once."

"Is the baby mine?"

Just then Geena slammed on the brakes doing 70 miles an hour. Screeching to a halt on the highway. My heart jumped through my chest and rested on the dashboard. After checking my body parts to see if I was still alive, I checked the back window to see how much traffic was behind us.   I was surprised to see the highway was empty except for a few cars.

"You selfish two timing hypocrite.   How dare you call me a whore to my face?"

"I didn't call you a whore.   I was asking a legitimate question."

I learned from that incident what women have known since the inception of time.   Don't pick a fight with the driver of the car.   I had broken women's rule number 3.

"Get out!"

"Get out? We are 65 miles from my house."

"Get! Out!"

"I ain't getting out."

"Oh, you are going to get out."

I had my chest puffed up, but I was kinda scared because I had no idea what Geena had planned.   Geena sped up and pulled off the highway.

"I ain't getting out.   I don't care what you do."

I was warning her of my defiant stand.   Just in case she thought I was joking.   When we got to the first stop light, I saw a huge sign pointing left to the Georgia State Patrol.   Geena turned left.

"Geena what are you doing?"

I didn't know what Geena had in mind but I was beginning to get nervous.   She pulled into the parking lot of the Georgia State Patrol, jumped out of the car and started screaming.

"HELLLPPPP!!!!!!   HELLLLPPPP!!!"

I jumped out on the passenger side.   "What are you doing?!"

"HELLLPPPP!!!!!!!!!!"

During the madness, I looked down the corridor and saw a patrolman running to the front of the building.   I was black, 60 miles from home, and in a country town in the south.   I didn't want any trouble.

"Okay! Okay!" I moved away from the car.

Geena jumped back in her BMW and sped off blowing gravel, dirt, and soot in my face. I spent the next three hours trying to convince the patrolmen not to investigate me and Geena's tirade. Like clockwork, I called V to come to pick me up. V showed up 2 hours later. A 4 hour trip had suddenly turned into a 10 hour excursion. V was cursing as I got in the car.

"Dude, we are getting too old for this."

"Hell, you're telling me."

"Do me favor? Don't talk to me all the way back to College Park."

Not a word was spoken all way back to our side of town. V didn't speak to me until I got out at my apartment.

"You need to check Geena's butt. That shit was ridiculous. Next time you going to be an 'In the country', Greyhound catching motherfucka."

I didn't even respond. I just closed the door and walked into the apartment. I came in, pulled up the laptop to check my emails. I stayed up for 3 hours putting some figures together for work the next day.

I didn't hear from Geena or Sandy the rest of the week. Usually I would have been stressed over not receiving any phone calls, but I needed a break. I had to focus on some stability. But I knew things were not going to be solid until the pregnancy situation was resolved. I knew Geena and I needed to talk. I didn't know why I was fighting the abortion issue, we were both in our thirties and the chances of Geena having an abortion were slim to none. Over the course of the next several days, I had reserved the fact that I was going to be a daddy. At least I wasn't alone. V was rolling down the same path. Maybe our children would be best friends by the fourth grade the way we were.

I used the weekend to rest. I knew I had a long week ahead of me at work and I wanted to tackle my situation with Geena as well. I sat around all weekend looking at football games and eating. Mike and Rich came over to

watch the Falcons game on Sunday. When Mike came over
he had a beer in his hand. He had bought the case earlier in
the week and kept it in his trunk. Tonya wouldn't allow him
to drink in their house. Rich came in and threw his leg over
the arm of the couch.

"What's up, bro?"

"What's happening man? Take your leg off the arm of
my couch. Is that the way white folks in Buckhead treat
their furniture?"

Rich pulled his leg down slowly trying to balance a leg
movement and sipping his brew.

"Why you got to play to the race card? I thought we
were bigger than that."

"Whatever. How did you all hook up?"

"He called me claiming Tonya was driving him crazy."

"He needs to stay home and watch those kids."

"Hell I do. What do you think I've been doing the
whole weekend? Where's Geena? She's usually over here on
Sundays."

I changed the subject.

"Who are the Falcons playing today anyway? I've been
so out of it."

"The Giants. This is Trotter's first game against his old
team."

Damn! Everywhere I turned I had issues. I hadn't
planned on drinking. Now I needed a brew. I grabbed a
brew from Mike's case and settled into the game.

Rich always played the odds, "I betcha Trotter has a
monster game."

I snapped back, "Why do you think that?"

"Against his old team. Shit. The Falcons are done."

I took Rich's bet and raised him. Trotter caught,
tackled, and destroyed everything in his path that day. The
camera came to the sideline for an interview.

"I'm in a new place, but the game remains the same. I
want to say hello to my mother. ...And I also want to put a

shout out to my baby. Be home in a minute."

I sat there and stared at the television. I knew he was talking about Sandy. The fellas and I drank another beer before they headed home.

I arrived at work and was called into a meeting first thing. Johnson was meeting with the whole staff.

"Gentlemen and Gentlewomen we have been asked to take a look at a job at the Auto Assembly Plant in Hapeville."

I spoke up.

"How big is this project, sir?"

"Ten million. I want you to head the Analysis. Richard...you are assistant project manager. They want to raise productivity by 15%."

Mike shouted, "At the Ford Plant? Yeah right. You aren't going to be able to do that. The union isn't going to allow it."

"We are going to look at the bottom line and make the recommendations but this account could lead up to another 100 million dollars." Johnson countered.

Everybody sat up. That would mean serious bonuses for everyone. Everyone's body language exhibited excitement and joy except Mike. Mike had worked in accounting at the plant before coming to the firm. All the consultants moved back to their cubicles to develop and research scenarios on how to improve the plant's productivity. Rich and I stayed behind to go over some numbers with Johnson. After leaving Johnson's office, I stopped by Mike's cubicle.

"Hey Man! I just got through talking to Johnson. If this thing goes off, it's going to be a $12,000 bonus for you."

"It's going to be like pulling teeth. The only way we are going to be successful is to cut heads."

"You don't know that."

"Dude, I worked there. I know."

Then it dawned on me what was bothering Mike. He

had left the plant on good terms with everyone. Now he was returning as the enemy. I told Mike to go home and relax. Everything was going to be okay. But I really didn't know if everything was going to be okay. Rich and I worked together the rest of the day to select several areas that would be productivity targets. I worked late into the evening and caught the train home. It was a quiet ride. I had time to gather my thoughts. Geena and I needed to talk about the pregnancy. Time was running out.

The next day, the consulting staff descended on the plant like a pack of wolves headed to a slaughter. We were motivated by visions of high-end bonuses dancing in our heads. That is...everybody except Mike. Mike proceeded with caution.

We set up meetings, then met with the management. I let Rich handle the presentation meeting. We introduced ourselves and split up into our specialized areas. I went to the meet with the superintendent, Rich went to operations, and Mike went to accounting. The rest of the staff met with the supervisors. At the end of the day, I got a page. It was Geena. I checked messages. She wanted to talk. I needed to talk, as well. There was a decision that needed to be made and we needed to make it. I called her back.

"Hello."

"How are you?"

"I'm okay. I see you made it back."

"I did. No thanks to you."

"You need to be thanking me that you weren't posting bail."

"Look. I'm not trying to fight with you. Can you meet me at my house?"

"No."

"You want me to come to your house."

"No. Why don't you meet me at the Salon?"

"I can do that."

After work, I took the ride to Geena's salon. In that

small amount of minutes, I played several scenarios and responses in my head. I was prepared. I was ready. My hesitancy to make the confrontation afforded me to be a few minutes late. As I turned into the parking lot of Geena's salon, my phone rang.

"Hello."

Sandy was calling at the wrong time

"We haven't talked in a few days. I was calling to say goodbye."

"So it's over like that?"

"Look. We gave it a shot. But we're two different people."

"So what kind of person are you and what kind of person am I?"

At that second, Geena walked to the front of the salon and saw my truck sitting in the parking lot. She looked at me, then pointed to her watch. I motioned back, "give me a minute." I went back to my phone conversation.

"Well what time are you leaving? Maybe I can see you before you go."

"I'm leaving in the morning. But it's a real busy time for me right now. This isn't something flowers are gonna cure."

"Well I guess you know about cures, Doc. Look I got to go into a meeting. I'll call you when I get out."

Reluctantly, Sandy agreed. We said goodbye. I wanted to see her one last time before she left Atlanta. I hung up and rushed into the salon. Geena was in her office ordering supplies. She continued ordering her products without looking me in the face. I wondered what she was thinking.

"For a minute, I didn't think you were coming in."

"I had to take that call."

"I'm sure you did. So I guess you want to talk about the baby."

"Yeah, we need to talk. I think you need to think this thing through."

"I've decided to get an abortion."

"Huh?"

"I decided to get an abortion."

Geena had defied all my expectations, but there was no rhyme nor reason why.

"So how did you come to this decision?"

I may have been asking a loaded question. As selfish as it was, I had always been told to never look a gift horse in the mouth. But I had to ask.

"Look. You don't want a baby and neither do I. At least not from you anyway." As much as I was supposed to be relieved, I was offended. Did she think she was better than me? ...That her genes were better than mine? I didn't like her tone.

"What's that suppose to mean?"

"Just what I said. We don't want a baby."

Then she baited me in like a fish on a hook.

"So you want a baby?"

"Huh. I didn't say that either."

"Well make up your mind."

"I did, Geena."

"Well What?! Make up your mind, damn it."

"Stop! You're confusing me!"

I had lost control of the conversation. Geena was toying with me like her personal Ken doll and I fell right into her little playhouse.

"Look Geena. I think we should go with the first choice. We made a decision, let's stick with it."

"Well, that's what we're gonna do."

Somehow I'd felt like Geena allowed me to make the decision. Allowing the guilt to roll down my back. Her eyes watered as she said, "That's what we're gonna do." Geena and I decided to go through with the procedure the next weekend. I stayed at Geena's salon with her until she finished her work. It gave me an opportunity to gage her emotions. I couldn't read her. She was emotionless. I thought her attitude was strange but I knew Geena wasn't

the type of person who would go down so easily. I told her
I had an appointment to make. But if she needed me to
come by her house later, I could. She said no. In fact, she
ordered me to go home. She told me that with an attitude
that said, "You better remember this is the last time. 'Cause
brother, you will never smell this pooh again." I gave her a
hug and told her I would call her tomorrow. She said okay.
But her body language told me she didn't care if I called her
or not. At this point, this was strictly a business deal.

I jumped into my truck and headed downtown to
Sandy's apartment.   I told her that I would be coming over
about 9 o'clock, but now it was close to 10:30. I didn't
know if she was still there or staying with one of her friends
while she engineered her move.   When I got there, a U-
Haul truck was parked outside her building. As I got out of
my truck, I looked up at Sandy's building and got a little
choked up. I knew I would pass this building a thousand
more times and the thought of Sandy not living here would
place a void in my heart. Already late, I rushed up to the
apartment. When I got to her doorway, I knocked but there
was no answer. I turned the knob. The door was open. I
walked in. Her apartment was clean. There were very few
things left to move. Suddenly I heard a sound. There was
a sound of wrapping in the back bedroom. A smile fell on
my face. She didn't hear me knock. I marched to the
bedroom.

"I knocked a hundred times. Why didn't you open the
door?"

The woman jumped up screaming. I had frightened her.
I quickly began to apologize.

"Hey! Hey! I'm sorry. I'm sorry. I'm a friend."

The white woman looked familiar to me. I looked
closer. It was Sandy's mother.

"Ms. Franklin?"

"Ooh. You scared me."

"I'm…"

"I know who you are. I've seen your picture."

"So I've been mentioned once or twice?"

"Definitely more than twice."

"You came all the way down here to help the Doc move?"

"She still needs her mom sometimes."

Sandy's mother was a keeper. She was a beautiful woman. I had underestimated her beauty from her picture. If I ran into her on the street and she wasn't Sandy's mother she would have definitely been in my cross hairs. Older woman or not.

"I see. Where is she?"

"She went to get some chicken wings. I told them I would keep working."

"Oh, somebody's with her?"

"Yeah. A friend of hers is helping her move. He plays football for some team."

When I heard Sandy's Mom say that I knew this wasn't the place I needed to be.

"Well, tell her I was coming through to tell her goodbye. Tell her to have a safe trip."

"I will. She should be back any second. You sure you don't want to wait?"

"No. No. It was a pleasure meeting you."

I headed for the door. Just then we heard people coming through the front door. I could hear the laughter escalating as Sandy walked through the door. She noticed me as she walked through the door. She paused as if she were an eight-year-old caught in her mother's makeup case. Kevin was with her. Unaware he was the center of drama, Kevin spoke up first.

"Frat!!"

I reluctantly greeted him.

"What's happening Frat?"

"You must have talked my girl into coming to NYC. Did you talk to her?"

"It was her decision, man. I tried to talk her into staying, so she wouldn't disturb your game. But she said she had to go."

"I'm glad she didn't take your advice. I play better when she's there."

When he said that, I got a swollen feeling in the pit of my stomach. All those Sundays I sat on my couch and praised him, he had used Sandy as his motivation to play better. I looked over at Sandy who was reluctant to make eye contact.

"I was just coming by to wish you a safe trip."

"Thank you. I'm almost ready."

Kevin cut the conversation short by making small talk.

"Wish you had been here an hour ago to help me with that heavy ass couch."

Sandy cut him off.

"Watch your mouth my mother's back there."

"Oh. I'm sorry."

"Well I'm going to get out of your way. Looks like you guys have everything under control."

"Well, it was good seeing you again Frat."

"You too Kevin."

I gave Sandy a fake half-hearted hug and headed for the door.

"Wait. I'll walk you to your truck."

I didn't respond and kept walking. As I got into the hallway, I heard Sandy pressing to catch up.

"Wait."

I kept walking.

"Why? You have things under control."

Sandy caught up with me pulling the back of my shirt to halt my progress. I stopped just to remove her hand from my shirt, which she picked up on immediately.

"Oh, it's like that?"

"Yeah. It's like that."

"Look. I didn't know Kevin was coming. He called and

said he was at the airport."

"...And you didn't invite him. Is that what I'm suppose to believe?"

"Believe what you want to. I'm telling the truth."

"Are you finished?"

"No. I'm gonna miss your butt."

My conscience told me to give in. But I couldn't go out like that.

"I'll miss you too. Take care. Bye."

I drove off. I looked at Sandy standing in my rearview mirror and wondered how could both of us come from a nuclear family foundation and carry on such a dysfunctional relationship. Sandy stood in the same spot as I turned the corner. Her body language looked as if she was waiting for me to circle the block and come back. Something I would have done 3 months ago. Not that day. I kept driving.

19 . . .

*T*he phone rang the next morning. I wasn't planning on answering it, but after hearing a recall seven times, I had no choice. It was V. He was calling me before he headed to work.

"Hello."

"Wake up Man!"

"Yeah I'm up. What you need?"

"I was calling to tell you. Marti and I set a date."

"That's good. Call me back in 3 hours and tell me when it is."

"Wake up. I want you to go help me pick out some tuxedos."

I was half awake and half asleep. My eyes still closed, the phone laid on top my face as I slurred responses to V's energized questions.

"Okay. Give me a call about 10 a.m. We'll set something up."

"Will do. Oh yeah. Some consultants just came into our plant..."

My eyes opened.

"Yeah?"

"A lot of people are worried about their jobs. I told them not to worry. My best friend was a consultant and it didn't work like that. I told them that I was going to talk to you and get some advice."

"Okay. Well we'll talk about it later today."

Within an hour and a half, I was out the door and headed to work. I drove to the assembly plant. Urban legend had long been spread that anyone that drove a foreign car into the parking lot of an American automotive assembly plant would not have their car long, because the employees would destroy it. They lived and breathed union and American Made. I didn't feel any threats about my car, seeing that mine was American. Rich drove a Range Rover though.

I reached the assembly plant about 8:15 and went straight into meetings with the superintendent.

"So, has your team come up with any results?"

"They're putting the numbers together as we speak."

"You promised me an improvement of 15%. That equals 20 million dollars. I want my 20 million dollars."

"You are going to get your 20 million. I promise."

"I'm going to hold you to that."

Superintendent Towns took me on his tour. His full name was Tommy Nathaniel Towns. The initials, TNT, and his attitude was like a piece dynamite. He toured the plant twice each day, during the 9 o'clock and 1 o'clock hours. He ruled the parts movement area with an iron fist. His supervisors would tell him anything to keep him off their asses. They supervised in fear. The employees didn't fear Towns because he couldn't talk to them the way he talked to his supervisors. The union didn't allow it. We made a stop at the bumper line.

"Are the blue bumpers on the line yet?"

The supervisor reluctantly came up with an answer. Even though she really didn't know.

"Not yet sir. Should be here in two minutes."

"Get your head out of your ass and get over there and move those bumpers!!"

"Yes sir! Yes sir!"   The supervisor didn't move fast

enough for Towns.

"Well move! Now!"

The assemblymen would laugh at the supervisor and Towns would move on. When he wasn't confronting a supervisor, Towns was calm.

"The only way they can do their job properly is fearing that I'm going to come around the corner at any time. That's the way you supervise. Fear is the key."

"Do you think that's the best way to do it?"

"Hell yeah!"

Towns was a good old boy from a small town 50 miles south of Atlanta. He had made an 100-mile trek each day knowing that his plant job would propel him farther than any job in High Falls, Georgia. Towns made more money than the mayor of High Falls.

Armed with little more than a high school education, Towns had built his own little kingdom behind the walls of the assembly plant. And he ruled it on fear. He had worked for Ford for thirty-two years. Two years longer than the average Ford employee, but at 50 he had a couple of years of his in-your-face style of management still left in him. He also knew the average employee died within five years after retirement and his fear of leaving the world too early kept him on the road making his pilgrimage each day at 4 a.m.

"Well, I think you should share your knowledge to train them to look for certain red flags within the operation."

"The only red flag they need to know is that their ass hole better be tight when they see me coming."

Towns believed that if his supervisors did their jobs correctly he would not have to belittle them in front of the people reporting to them. If they didn't, they got what they deserved. What Towns had failed to realize was the supervisors were caught between two worlds. He couldn't manage by intimidation. He had to garner the respect of his employees first. Most of the plant's supervisors managed somewhere between the respect factor and a fear of the boss.

I made a mental note that the first workshop we would hold would be Management Styles. Towns needed it.

After the tour, I went back to the war room. Mike was there working on the figures from accounting and purchasing. He looked weary.

"What's wrong?"

"The only way I see us getting to 15% is a reduction of 12,000 hours a week."

"About 25 people?"

"30 people."

"You sure?"

"Look at the numbers for yourself."

I checked Mike's numbers. He was right. The only way we could get to 20 million dollars was to recommend a layoff of 30 people.

"Where are we seeing the cuts coming from?"

"Looks like 15 people from the assembly line, 10 from Parts Control, and 5 from the Body Shop."

"The Body Shop? You sure?"

"You see it. You got the numbers in front of you. What's the big deal with the Body Shop?"

"My best friend works in the Body Shop."

"How long has he been there?"

"About 3 years."

"He's gone, man. This will get him."

"Fuck!"

Just then my pager went off. It was V telling me he'd meet me at the tuxedo store at Southlake Mall around 6. I didn't respond back, but he knew his message went through.

I arrived at the mall early in the evening. I'd spent most of the day running the numbers. The staff and I kept coming up with the same outcome. Let 30 people go. As I came through Sears, I contemplated telling V in confidence what I had come up with. I asked myself, was it my place to tell him or was it Ford's? I didn't know, so I decided to play it by ear.

As I walked up to the store, I could see the excitement on V's face. He had already started trying on tuxedos. I concluded this wasn't the time for confidential conversations. I walked into the store. V turned around flossing his FUBU tuxedo.

"Boy, you are just like a kid. You can't wait for anything."

V was proud of his taste in formalwear.

"How you like me now?"

"Not bad. How many tuxes have you tried on?"

"This is the first one. You're just in time."

"Which ones have you set up for me?"

"The ones with the ruffles over there."

"Crack kills, son. Crack kills."

The sales girl started laughing. V spoke up.

"Oh so you like his jokes, huh?"

"That was funny."

Her southern drawl bounced heavily off the walls of the store. Her dialect told me she lived a lot further past Atlanta's suburban landscape. After hearing her voice, I decided to quiz her.

"Where are you from?"

"Griffin."

Griffin was small town about 60 miles south of Atlanta.

"...And you sound like it. Just jokes."

"So you want to see the ruffles?" She asked getting back to business.

"Nooo...Let me see the Versaces."

V interrupted our conversation.

"You got Versace money?"

"You don't know nothin' bout me."

"I see. I see. Do your thang. Oh yeah. I saw a card from one of the consultants. I could have sworn it was your firm."

"It is...that's a good looking shirt. I think you should go with that one."

"You do?"

It was a delayed reaction but he realized I had answered his question.

"Say what? When were you going to tell me that? I can tell my boy's in the shop, we don't have anything to worry about."

I didn't want to answer any more questions at that point. I wanted to go home.

"No. I guess not."

Now I really wanted to crawl under a rock. I wondered how V would judge me in a couple of months. V continued trying on tuxedos and making conversation.

"Do you know the person in charge of the project?"

"Yeah I know him."

"What's his name? I got to look out for y'all? Nothing personal, but you can't trust consultants."

"You trust me, right?"

"Yeah, but we've got history."

I wondered to myself, for how long?

V picked out the tux's for his ceremony. He picked 3. Now he had to take the sample cards home to Marti for final approval. V talked me into having dinner with him at Ruby Tuesday's. His treat. During dinner, I let V in on consulting insight. If you see us coming, make sure you are working. It had been a part of the UAW culture, not to let management or consultants intimidate them. But this was a new generation, the country was in a recession and there was a new sheriff in town. Me. After dinner, I rushed home to re-work those numbers again. V had been there for me so many times. I couldn't let him down now. I knew I was embarking on a short journey that could hold a friendship together or tear it apart.

The next day I returned to the office, planning to work there the rest of the week. I let Mike and Rich work with staff and hold the workshops we'd developed. Rich called me on Thursday to tell me he felt Towns had undermined his authority during one of the workshops. He said he wasn't holding another workshop with Towns present. I assured Rich that I would have a conversation with Towns first thing.

I came back to the plant on the last day of the week. I called Towns before I got there to set up a meeting. I didn't define the agenda over the phone. I didn't want to give him a chance to align supporters. I got to Towns's office around mid-morning.

"Knock, knock."

"Come on in. Have you made me a couple of million yet?"

"Not yet sir."

"I'm waiting on my millions."

I didn't respond to Towns's statement.

"Mr. Towns?"

"Call me Tom."

"Tom. Rich told me you kept interrupting his workshop yesterday?"

"Yeah. I had to correct him on a couple of things. Did he ask you to come in and thank me?"

"No. Not really. That's what I'm here to talk to you about."

Towns was reading memos and talking at the same time but stopped when I mentioned trouble.

"What was said?"

"Nothing to be alarmed about."

"Well why do I feel like I need to be alarmed?"

"Calm down. Rich felt like you were cutting him off during the workshop. All I want to ask you to do is allow Rich do the job he is being paid to do."

When I said that, I could see the blood rushing to Towns's face. I had imposed on his power. I had stepped on his toes. He looked like skinny Santa Claus.

"Listen here, you Breast Milk Sucking-Just out of College-No Idea how to Run a Business Motherfucker..."

"Hey! Hey! I'm not here to get into a confrontation with you. All I want you to do is let Rich do his job."

"I ain't doing nothing. If I think he doesn't know what he's talking about, I'm gonna cut his ass off."

"No you aren't."

"I will have your ass out of here tomorrow."

Towns picked up the phone and started dialing. I figured he would call the plant manager, so I made the call before I walked into Towns's office. Towns screamed at his assistant to get the plant manager on the phone.

"Jim! I need to talk to you."

His conversation went from aggressive to tempered to down right meek. The first half of the conversation, Towns attempted to stare me down. By the end of the second half, I had nicknamed him Tigger.

"Yeah. We'll talk later."

Towns hung the phone up.

"Get out of my office."

"I can do that. But I sure would appreciate it if you'd tone it down at the next workshop. I'll take it, you'll be there."

"Get...Out."

"I'm out. Have a good weekend."

I smiled and as I left the office. I called Rich after the meeting to let him know everything was under control and he shouldn't expect any more trouble from TNT.

THICKER THAN WATER

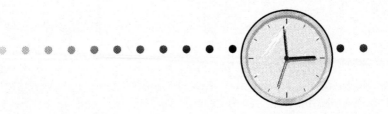

20 . . .

I got over to Geena's house early Saturday morning. Something about that morning seemed off. It was like I had left my body and was watching my movements from outside looking down like an out-of-body experience. I've never felt that feeling before nor have I felt it since.

"How are you doing this morning?"

"As well as can be expected."

"You want to stop at McDonald's and get something to eat?"

"No. They said they didn't want me to eat 12 hours before."

Geena had mentally separated herself from even saying the word abortion.

"Maybe we can eat afterwards?"

"I'm not going to want to eat afterwards."

Right now Geena was in charge and I didn't want to rock her boat. My small talk didn't seem to be helping the situation.

"Where are we going?"

Never looking up, Geena handed me the directions and her keys. She decided I'd drive her car so she wouldn't have to step up into my truck when we to left the clinic. It was a slow quiet drive to our final destination. Geena brought

a throw-blanket with her. She covered herself and turned her
back to me staring out into the black of early morning. I
thought I would reach over and place my hand on her back
to show my support for the decision. As soon as she felt my
touch, she shrugged my hand off her shoulder. I was so
confused. Was I doing the right thing? Was I forcing Geena
to do something she didn't want to do? I didn't know.
Then I told myself that if there were any doubts, this was
the best thing. I turned the radio on to pacify the energy
between us. The first station that came up was gospel.
Gospel...right now? The second station was contemporary
gospel. I quickly changed before I had an uprising on my
hands.

The third station was a pre-recorded sermon from one of
the old school Atlanta ministers. I could hear the
worshipers in the background saying, "Preach, brother,
preach." I turned the radio off. Atlanta had 3 major R&B
stations and all of them were playing gospel on a Saturday
morning. What was really going on? I guess it was God's
way of saying, "I'm just trying to help you out in your
situation."

We arrived at the clinic at the break of dawn. I didn't
know what to expect, as a consultant I had always been
taught to do my research before green-lighting a task. With
so much going on, I let this slip through the crack. The
parking lot was filled to capacity. I had no idea how
common the procedure was. Geena grabbed her purse and
started for the door. For a second, I sat behind the steering
wheel thinking. About what, I didn't know. I was trying to
think about something. Something positive. Anything but
this. It was a feeble attempt to block out what was about
to go down. But my mind was blank of new images. The
old ones stood fast. After about 10 steps, Geena noticed I
wasn't behind her. I could read her lips through the glass.
"Are you coming or what?" I shook my head yeah, got out
and followed. Two minutes later we were at the door behind

6 half-sleepy couples and 2 sets of parents. The hold-up was due to an Atlanta Police officer checking women's bags and frisking the men as if we were entering to a nightclub. Then it hit me. The last thing the doctor needed was a civil unrest inside the clinic. I complied with my body check just like everybody else.

When we got upstairs, I was shocked at all the blank stares and restless energy floating in the room. Women were filling out medical history forms while their mates looked around at the other males in the room wondering what was the next man's story. We were joining a fraternity, one that we wouldn't promote nor would we be proud of. I looked at my watch every ten minutes as the women in the room disappeared one after another. An hour into our journey, a nurse appeared from behind the big brown door.

"Regeena Gordon."

Geena had fallen asleep resting her head on my shoulder. She wearily heard her name through her drowsiness. She placed her purse in my lap and walked to the back as if she was a prisoner accepting her sentence. I reached out to touch her hand before she went back but she saw me and avoided my touch like the plague. I looked around to see if anybody noticed. All were watching, just like I had when it was their turn. I knew they wondered the details of my story. I picked up one of a thousand magazines and started to read. I could tell the tattered Sports Illustrated had passed through a thousand hands before me. I went from Sports Illustrated to People to Us to Glamour. Slowly my eyelids abandoned me and before I knew it my eyes were closed and the sheep had retired.

In my sleep, I could still hear the big brown door open and close, one after another. People were leaving and trying to bring their lives back to some semblance of normality. For some of the men, a sense of relief was released from their shoulders when they saw their mates walk out of the procedure room. Especially the fathers of the teenagers who were determined not to alter their daughters' seemingly perfect lives. But it was too late, these women would never be the same. Something had been removed from their bodies, but it would remain stamped on their soul forever. Whether it was their decision or someone else's.

The door opened and closed so many times, I had accounted for the noise in my sleeping pattern. What I didn't account for was the loud scream I heard after an hour of good sleeping. I wiped my eyes, sat up and struggled through my stupor to see what was happening. Through the haze, I could see the front office nurses rushing to the back.

All of a sudden, the nurse rushed through the door.

"Is Regeena Gordon's party here?!"

I raised my hand like I was in school and scared to answer the question. The nurse spotted me.

"Can you come with me please?!"

As I jumped up, I heard another scream. As fast as I was rushing to the back, several scenarios were rushing through my head. I was praying that Geena was okay. How was I going to explain this to her mother? Before I could get to the room, I saw a nurse bum rushing the room followed by reinforcements. I suddenly grew upset and came to Geena's defense.

"What did you do to her?!"

"Calm down!" The nurse ordered.

"No. You hurt her! What'd you do?"

Before the staff could realize the magnitude of the situation, they had two out of control people on their hands. I could hear Geena screaming from behind the wall and I was trying to get to her. The doctor came from Geena's room to investigate the ruckus in the hallway.

"Hey! Hey! Calm down!"

"What's going on?!" I shouted again.

"She's fighting through the medicine."

"What do you mean, she's fighting through the medicine?"

The doctor led me into the examination room. There was Geena, lying on the table fighting four nurses.
"So you've finished the procedure?"
"We haven't started the procedure."
"Seriously?"
"Seriously."
I looked at Geena putting up a fight.
"Don't let them take my baby! Please don't let them take my baby!"
I leaned over Geena to calm her down. I grabbed her hand and sat next to her where she could see me. I really didn't know if she knew it was me, but I needed to let her know I was there.
"Geena, it's me. I'm here with you."
I could see Geena fighting through the medicine. I looked at her eyes. They were moving a thousand miles an hour as if she were fighting not to fall asleep. Out of the corner of her eye fell a tear. A tear for help. Even with anesthesia soaked in her bloodstream, Geena was still trying to protect her baby and garner support. When the staff thought they had Geena sedated, the doctor pulled me into the hallway.
"I need to ask you to make a decision."
"Me? Why me?"
"Ms. Gordon's under sedation. She filled out the request to complete the procedure, but it appears as if she's changing her mind. It could be her or it could be the medicine. She signed you as her point of contact."
It had all come back to me. Why me? Why was I making the decision? Why did I have to be the one who had to endorse this life altering experience? I thought back to Geena originally asking me the question, the radio stations playing the gospel, the expressions on everyone's faces when we walked into the clinic. The doctor looked to me for answers. I looked to the sky for one. I wanted to ask if we could come back and try it again tomorrow, but I knew that

wasn't an option.

"We're going home. I can't do it."

"You sure?"

"Yes sir. We're going home."

At that point my spirit descended back into my body. I walked back into the procedure room. Geena had fallen asleep. She laid there exhibiting this invisible strength, even through her sleep. She had attempted to sway the jury and they listened. I sat next to her. I could see her rapid eye movement through her eyelids. She was resting, but she wasn't really relaxing. I touched her hand, she clutched my hand back. I looked up to see if she was awake. Her eyes were still closed. I watched as another tear rolled down the side of her face.

An hour later, we were on our way back to Geena's place. As fast as we could get in the car, Geena had reclined her seat and was sleeping again. When we arrived at the house, I put on some jazz and let it lighten her mind while she slept. Still under a light sedation, I undressed Geena and put her to bed. I decided to lay down beside her and be there in case she needed me.

As evening broke, I could hear the birds chirping as if they were alerting all-comers that this was the last call before the flock headed south. I cleared the water breaking from the corner of my mouth and cracked my eyes. Geena was awake and staring at me. My first thought was, "How long have you been awake? ...And why are you staring at me?"

"You okay?"

When I said that, the stare became a frown and the frown became a cry.

"You let them kill my babyyyyy."

Geena started pounding against my shoulders and chest. I grabbed her arms to restrain her. After a little bit of resistance, she gave in and began to cry on my shoulder. I realized then, she didn't recall what happened.

"No. No I didn't. You didn't follow through."

She suddenly looked up into my eyes. She was searching for truth.

"I didn't?"

"Nope. In fact they told us not to bring our asses back."

After hearing that she let out a half-hearted laugh which turned back into a cry. This time it was a cry of relief. At one point she was crying and laughing at the same time. She suddenly felt her stomach and looked at me.

"I'm hungry now."

21

I spent the rest of the weekend at Geena's house. I was her personal slave for the weekend. I made a couple of sandwiches, watched a couple of football games, and fetched 103 glasses of orange juice. Geena and I had come to a silent understanding without uttering a word that a baby was on the way. I think Geena used my sympathy for all it was worth. By Sunday night I was asking her, "Anything else Your Hind Ass?" She just laughed and said, "I'll let you know."

After a long weekend, I rotated back to my other trade. I was back at the plant. Rich had held a workshop earlier that morning. I stopped by to see how things were going. Rich held a good workshop with no interruptions. Towns had moved from the second row to standing in the back. Even in compliance, he would still remain defiant in his own way. We made eye contact but there was no conversation involved. When we got back to the office, Mike and Rich quizzed me on my Friday meeting with Towns.

Mike asked, "What did you do to Towns? He was meek as a lamb."

"We had a small conversation. I felt it was very positive."

Rich joined in, "It was more than positive. He didn't say

a word."

"Hell. That's good. If he listens a little, maybe he will pick up some things he doesn't know."

Mike said, "Trust me. You haven't heard the last from Towns. I worked with the man for 5 years."

"We'll see."

I decided to take a tour of the plant by myself this time. As I walked around, I could see the recommendations were having a positive effect on operations at the plant. People were working and stock was getting to the assembly line. I stopped and had a few conversations with a couple of the supervisors. As I walked through bumpers, the supervisor stopped me.

"Can I talk to you for a second?"

"Yes. What do you need?"

"I just wanted to thank you."

"Thank me for what?"

"Talking to Towns. I don't know how long it's going to last, but he's definitely not the same person he was last week."

"Who said I talked to Towns?"

"Are you kidding? The whole plant knows about it."

"I don't know what you're talking about?"

"Okay. Whatever you say. But thank you anyway. I can do my job now."

I winked at her.

"Just make sure those bumpers get to the line."

"I will."

I continued on my tour. I stopped by the bulletin board to read a memo.

To: Management Staff
From: Human Resources
Subject: Questions on New Procedures

Many of you have had questions over the last several days

about new processes and procedures being implemented. Please direct those questions to your supervisor or Malik Douglass, Richard Cooke, or Michael Vines of the Smith and Boland consulting group.

Karen Robbins
Human Resources

I thought to myself, good directive. About 15 minutes later, I'd made my way to the body shop. When I got there, there was nothing going on. I noticed V in the corner. He was engaged in shoptalk with the fellas. In fact, V was leading the story. His arms were waving. I could tell it was one of the best jokes he had ever told. If we weren't at work, I would have been over there getting my laugh on too. But this was work. V turned around to see who had entered the room. We made eye contact. V saw me then turned around and continued to tell his story. As if I wasn't there. He didn't even acknowledge me. Defiance of authority was running rampant in the plant. From top to bottom. Damn!

I walked into the supervisor's office.

"How are you doing? Is there any work to do in the shop?"

The supervisor looked up reading his morning copy of the Atlanta Constitution.

"...And you would be?..."

"The Project Manager for the consulting group."

"Oh."

He jumped up and acted like something was more important than the Living Section. At that given second, I understood Towns's management style. I wasn't saying it was right, I'm saying I understood.

"Yeah. There are a couple of things we could be doing."

"Let's take a look at them. I wouldn't want the plant manger to walk in and see the guys in the corner telling jokes. Not a good thing."

As I walked out of the shop, I could hear the shopmen cursing. I was messing up their good thing. Most of them had worked on the line for 20 years or more. This was their time to take it to the ranch. Relax a little bit. I understood that. But relax mode wasn't going to get me to the 20 million I promised Ford. They were one of the big reasons why we had to cut so many hours. Overtime in the Body Shop.

I stepped back into the office. Mike had missed lunch and was working on moving some numbers. Mike was good at moving numbers and shifting a business focus.

"What are you going to tell me? We're expanding the business?"

"Shit, contracting the business is more like it."

"No changes huh."

"Nope. Body Shop is going to be the hardest hit. There are too many spent hours and not enough work going through there."

"Can we hold it another week before we make a recommendation?"

"Yeah. But it's going to be close. Another week and we're going to have to work our asses off."

"That's what we get paid for."

"That's what you say. I got 3 kids to go home to."

At that moment, I got a page. No name, just a number. It was coming from the plant. It must have been Towns. I picked up the phone, dialed the number hoping to recognize the voice. There was a pickup on the other end.

"Hello."

"Did someone just page me?

"Yeah. I did."

"V?"

"Yeah. It's me. What do you think you're doing?"

"What do you mean?"

"How do think you're just going to come on our turf and tell us how to do our job?"

"First of all, I was talking to the supervisor.   Secondly, what job? You were telling jokes. Now if this is the comedy club, let me know. I'll buy a ticket."

"We get a hell of a lot of work done down here!"

"When? When it's convenient? On overtime?"

"Dude, you're swimming above your head here."

"V, trust me. Go back to work. We'll talk about this later."

"I want to talk about it now."

I hung up on him. He pissed me off. He was trying to play bad ass in front of his shop buddies. I could tell by his voice he had told them he had the inside track and now he was trying to save face. The phone rang again. I didn't answer it. I left the office, headed back downtown and told Mike not to worry about answering the phone for the rest of the day.

When I got back to the office, I had a message. Johnson wanted to see me with the preliminary figures for the project. I checked in. He told me he wouldn't be available until 2. Two was good for me. It gave me an opportunity to finalize the numbers. After lunch, I rolled into Johnson's office armed and ready. When I got to the office, he was still on the phone. He invited me in. I strolled over to the window to look out. As I looked out of the corner office on the 45th floor, I wondered how long it would be before I had my view overlooking Woodruff Park. Johnson had a telescope in his office. Curiously I peeked through. It was a view worthy of an executive. I made a mental note. Get a high rise office. Get a telescope.

"How's the project going? Have a seat."

"Pretty good."

"I hear you have some problems with Towns?"

"A small one, but that's nipped. How did you find out about that?"

"Rich told me."

"It got handled."

"Good to hear."

"How are we looking? Saved $40,000 last week."

"Where did we need to be?"

"80,000."

"Well, what are we doing about it?

"We need to cut heads."

"Are you sure?"

"Yes sir, they are 1,200 over in hours each week."

"You got the numbers?"

"Right here."

"Let me see."

Johnson mulled over the numbers, checking each column. I had double checked them 3 times, which meant 6. The problem was the firm had promised the plant that layoffs wouldn't be an option, and here we were right in the middle of a recommended layoff. The firm had under analyzed the project and promised the plant a check that our asses couldn't cash.

"Damn. Who else knows about this?"

"Just me, you, Rich and Mike."

"Keep it tight. Don't tell anyone. I'll work this out."

I complied and handed the problem over to Johnson. I figured Johnson would refigure my calculations, have another meeting with the plant manager, and back off the $20,000,000 guarantee. In the meantime, I cleared my desk and headed home.   On the way I called Geena.

"What are you doing?"

"Recovering."

"Recovering from what? You didn't do anything."

"I got morning sickness."

"At 5 p.m.?"

"Leave me alone. I'm having a baby."

"Do your thang. I don't want no trouble."

"Are you coming over?"

"I'll call you. I need to talk to V about something."

"Okay. I'll expect your phone call."

By the time I got home and got out of the shower, my
phone was ringing off the hook. I knew it was V. It was a
V ring. I decided I would put on some drawers before I
dealt with him. After 3 calls, he apparently gave up. I
nuked a Gorton's Fish Filet and batched some mayo and
relish for some homemade tartar sauce and poured a glass of
Courveiser straight. I needed it. I was ready to chow
down. Just as I sat down, there was a whack on my door.

"What the...?!"

I looked through the peephole and there was V, still
puffed up. I opened the door. He barged in like he had
something to prove.

"What man?" I sighed.

"Oh you think we're suppose to just go back to work
because you said so?"

"V, I'm not about to argue with you over bullshit. If you
don't want to work. Don't."

"The shit isn't that easy. I know you like the back of my
hand."

"True. I'm holding the supervisor accountable. If y'all
don't support him, he'll probably be out."

"That's fucked up. That's really fucked up."

"Dude, the company is losing money with all that
overtime you all are clocking. Be realistic. That work can
be done between 6 and 3."

"I'm not here to talk about work."

"What'd you come over for?"

"To tell you not to drive to work. I'll pick you up
tomorrow. They are planning to fuck your truck up."

As pissed off as V was, he was still trying to look out.

"Don't worry about me. I'll get there. Sit down and
have a brew."

"I don't have time, Marti and I are picking out dresses
today."

V left. As quickly as he had marched in, he was gone
and I was thinking that working was the last thing he

needed to be worrying about. Not working was the big issue. After finishing my dinner, I trekked over to Geena's. When I got there, she was sitting on the living room couch wearing a pair of smiley face boxers and a 'wife-beater'. She was watching TV and eating a pint of Hagen-Daas Pineapple-Coconut with Van Camp's Pork-n-Beans.

"This is so good. Want some?"

"No. In fact you're making me sick and why are you eating beans out of the can?"

"They're good that way."

Geena was happy. I could feel her energy. Happiness was oozing from her pores. Even without a ring, the pregnancy was filling her thirst for love and companionship.

I was still unaware of where our relationship was heading. I hadn't asked any questions. We played couple for the next few weeks. Coming home to dinner everyday was something I had never experienced dating anyone. Though I wasn't ready to admit it. It did feel good. Especially with the stress on the job. I'd walked in to the smell of baked chicken and broccoli casserole. In eight years, Geena's behavior was noticeably different. She hadn't cooked for me two days in a row in the eight years we had dated. My apartment had become an abandoned cave. One evening just as I was settling into my meatloaf and mashed potatoes she popped the question.

"Isn't the lease at your apartment up soon?"

I hesitated.

"Yeah..."

"I was thinking why don't you put your stuff in storage and move in with me."

I thought to myself, "Why are you trying to trap me?"

"I'll think about it."

"What's there to think about? You're over here every night. Why pay rent?"

I wondered to myself when did this all come about? But unbeknownst to me and nobody else's fault, I had become a husband and father weeks ago. At that moment, my cell phone rang. The caller-ID showed V's number.

"It's V. Let me get that."

"Tell him I said hello."

I hit the talk button.

"Hello."

"Where have you been? I've been looking for you for a couple of days."

"I've been splitting time between downtown and the plant."

"I'm talking about your house. I've been over there twice. Where have you been sleeping?"

"Oh. I've been over Geena's."

"Tell Geena. I said, What's up? Tell her I need a haircut."

An obvious joke, V went bald 3 years ago.

"Have you gotten your final fitting for your tux?"

"No. I hadn't had a chance."

"The tux store is calling me saying they can't reach you."

"I'll get by there tomorrow."

"You better. Or you are going to get the midget version."

"I'll get by there tomorrow."

"How's Marti?"

"Getting fat."

"You put the pounds on."

"That doesn't mean she ain't fat."

Both of us spoke as one voice.

"It is, what it is!!"

Geena was looking at me like I was crazy. I had forgotten to tell her that Marti was pregnant too. V and I hung up. Geena let the conversation go, but I knew it would come up again soon.

"Did I tell you Marti is having a baby too?"

"Is she? I saw her and V at the mall about a month ago. She didn't say anything about it."

"Yeah. They told me they saw you."

Geena had that look in her eye. "You never brought up that you all had talked about me."

"It wasn't a big deal. They said they talked to you. That was it."

The conversation ended that abruptly. I was waiting for her to bring the move-in topic up again, but she didn't. I wanted to be there for her, but I didn't want to move in. I didn't know if it was because I wanted to hold on to my sacred bachelorhood or a twisted belief that Sandy was coming back. At that moment, I tried to end all conversation. I didn't want her to bring up anything related to Sandy. But I still wondered how she knew about Sandy. I knew that I hadn't been right in two years, but I thought I had been careful. Thinking back, I recalled rule 67. Never doubt a woman's intuition. I decided to come clean. "They're getting married too." I threw that out there and dipped back into my mashed potatoes. Geena was still talking about her seeing V and Marti at the mall. It must have clicked in about thirty seconds later. She got quiet. Her brain housing group was processing the information that had just been fed. She nonchalantly got up from the table. I got another bite of meatloaf as a just-in-case measure. She put her plate in the sink. She walked over picked up my plate, dumped my meatloaf and mashed potatoes in the garbage and put my plate in the sink.

"Geena, why did you do that?"

"Oh. I'm sorry. I thought you were finished."

"You know I wasn't finished."

"You were when you told me that."

Geena turned and headed for her bedroom. She stopped and turned back to me before she broke the crack of the door jam.

"I think this is a good night for you to sleep at home."

Then she turned and proceeded to her bedroom. Geena's body language told the story, even though she wasn't ready to put up a fight then. She was putting things into perspective. She was disappointed. Probably more disappointed in me. My best friend's girlfriend had become pregnant and he felt they should get married. Was she not worthy of the same respect? But I looked at it as four different people and two different situations.

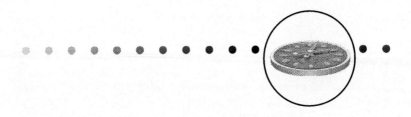

22 . . .

got to work the next morning about 8:15. Before I could get in the door good, Johnson was calling a meeting. I had just enough time to put my coat down and grab a pen and pad. Neither Rich, Mike, nor I had received exact details on the meeting seeing that the project had been going smoothly over the last couple of days. We were not where we needed to be, but we were further than we had been.

"I'm calling this meeting this morning to let all of you know, I think you've been doing a hell of a job."

All of us replied in unison.

"Thank you."

"I've gotten word from the plant manager and Detroit that we are going to proceed with the recommended layoffs."

Mike and I looked at each other. As if to say I don't believe this shit. I spoke up quickly.

"The layoffs, sir. Are you sure?"

I wondered about the layoffs because it had been a lapse in judgement on our part from the start, not the plant's.

"We showed him the plant projections and he agreed to them. Now our job will be to run the projections out to the superintendents. The plant manager will back us up after we roll them out. Gentlemen, your job will be the roll out."

Johnson said.

After the meeting, we grabbed a burger from the Varsity and headed back to the plant. I knew what was on Mike's mind, the same thing that was on mine. The last thing we were looking to do was recommend layoffs. Mike told me I wasn't finished with Towns. I had to discuss the layoff with him. When we got to the plant, an emergency meeting was held to strategize how we were going to lay off 30 people.

When I came to the firm, Johnson told me, "Remember, we don't lay people off. We only make the recommendation." He looked at it that way because it was easier for him to swallow when people lost their jobs. I thought about Johnson's advice and somehow it didn't make it any easier for me. This was going to be the first time the word layoff would be coming directly from my mouth to the client. I didn't feel pleased. I didn't feel fulfilled. I didn't feel satisfied. I had taken a look into the faces of the workers as they came back from their breaks. They looked happy and satisfied. For a lot of people, the assembly plant was hard work. But in a way, this was their American dream. They could ascend to the middle and upper middle class even if their education didn't exceed high school. Whether they were a drop out, had a high school education, or a college degree, they were a union. They got paid the same.

I called Towns and left a message on his voicemail saying that we needed to talk. I didn't tell him what the conversation was about. Towns was one of those people that you always had to have the upper hand, because you couldn't read him. The deck needed to be stacked on your side just to keep him off balance. But I suspected he would probably know before I met with him. Mike told me that rumors spread around the plant like wildfire. By the end of the day I had gotten a message from Towns saying he could meet with me first thing the next morning. Rich, Mike and I decided to pack it in for the day. We waited until the morning shift left and then the three of us stormed the parking lot. We were walking on a casual stroll and talking when Rich looked up.

"What the f....?"

Rich's voice was suddenly drowned out by the Delta 747 landing at the airport just over the plant's hilltop. But I knew from the first part of Rich's sentence and his body language that the situation needed immediate attention. Rich started running toward the cars.

Mike and I quickly looked out into the parking lot. I responded, " What?" I focused my line of sight in the direction Rich was running. Then I saw what Rich saw.

"What the fuck!?"

Our cars were trashed. The tires were flattened. The doors were keyed. In my paint, had been scribbled "Pig and Bird Dog". Bird Dog, a union term used for somebody who constantly watches the workers. Mike had 2 bullet holes in his front windshield. Rich was pacing back and forth cursing.

"I can't believe this shit! This is bullshit!"

Mike didn't say a word. He just walked over, sat on the curb, lit a cigarette and shook his head. I tried to calm the situation.

"Calm down. This type of stuff happens from time to time."

Rich had always been low-key and cool. Not today. He was pissed off, irate, and ready to fight.

"Calm down?! This isn't a '78 Volkswagen. It's a Range Rover!"

"I know you're upset."

"Upset ain't the word. Just in case you're trying to read my mind, tomorrow somebody might be missing some kneecaps."

I had to calm Rich down. He was getting more and more livid. "We aren't bringing guns to work. It's against regulations."

"Against regulations! Against regulations! What are you talking about? What kind of holes do you think those are in Mike's windshield?! BBs?"

Mike was still sitting on the curb staring into space. He hadn't said a word. I threw my hands up on Rich and walked over to see if Mike was okay. I looked over my shoulder and shouted back to Rich. "Go get security." Rich reluctantly walked off pouting like he was 10. He'd stop, look back at his truck about every 30 steps and start cursing again. I sat down the curb to get Mike's view, which wasn't too pleasant from my perspective either.

"You okay?"

Mike started talking but still made no eye contact with me.

"I was wondering. How am I going to explain bullet holes to my wife?"

"Tell her I borrowed it at lunch to go see one of my women and her husband came home."

"No. I'm serious dude. She didn't want me coming back to the plant because of shit like this to begin with."

I was trying to pull some wisdom from my back pocket to share with him. But I had none. He had the bullet holes in his car. What could I say that would make him feel better? Nothing.

Rich came back with the security guard, a fat white guy with a scruffy beard that looked like he lived for the Chick-fil-A sandwiches that were being served at the Dwarfhouse Restaurant across the street from the plant.

"So what happened here?"

By this time, I was a little irritated.

"We don't know. That's what we're asking you to investigate."

"Don't get testy with me. What did y'all do to these people anyway?"

Rich stepped up again.

"Do to these people! Dude. Those are bullet holes in

case you didn't notice."

"Oh. I noticed. These people don't mess with you unless you mess with them." He pulled out his pad and started taking his statement. "What department do y'all work in?"

"We don't work in any department. We work for a consulting firm."

"Oh so you all are the consultants."

"What do you mean? You all are the consultants."

"Nothing really. I just heard you guys were on the property."

"What did you hear?"

"Let's get this over with. I don't have all day."

"What did you hear?"

"I said, I ain't got all day. Gimme your statements."

Rich said. "Whatever. Give him the statements." We lined up and gave him our statements and information. Even though we somehow knew nothing was going to be done. Mike called Tonya to pick him up. Rich called Roadside assistance. They brought him a courtesy Range Rover. He took me home. I had my car towed to the nearest Ford dealership.

I gave Geena a call when I got home, but there was no answer. I didn't leave a message, she was probably still at the salon. I figured I'd call there. She answered the phone as if she was doing a million things and only had two hands.

"Geena's!" She shouted talking over the music.

"How are you feeling today?!" I shouted back even though I wasn't shouting over anything.

"Why are you hollering?!" Geena screamed back.

"I don't know. Because you are!"

She asked somebody in the background to turn the music down. The music suddenly went to a more even tone.

"Now what were you saying?"

"I was asking how you were feeling, but the party told the story."

"One of my stylists does a new singer's hair from ShoNuff Records and we were listening to some of her tracks."

"Sounds like you're in a little better mood than last night."

"I am. I went out for lunch and bought some new shoes for the wedding."

"The wedding?"

"Yeah. Marti and V's wedding."

"Oh. So you're going?"

"Yeah. I can't have the maid of honor thinking that she has a date."

"Right. Right."

"You don't have a problem with that, do you?"

"No. Noooo. You're welcome to come."

"I know I am. You sound like something is wrong."

"No. Not really."

"Not really means something is a wrong."

"Someone busted my windows, keyed my truck, and slashed my tires."

"Is there anything you want to tell me?"

"They did it at the plant."

"You okay? Have you called V?"

"No not yet. I just got home."

"You want me to come over? I only have one more client."

"You can. I'm tired, I'll probably be asleep by the time you get here."

We said goodbye, but never really confirmed whether she was coming over or not. I took a shower and went to bed. A couple of hours later, during one of my inner-sleep position changes I realized that I wasn't in my bed alone. Geena had slipped into my bed like a thief in the night. As I turned over, she opened her eyes. We laid there silently looking at each other for a few minutes. I began to speak. I wanted to ask how long she had been at my house, but before I could utter a word, Geena took her fingers pressed them against her lips, then touched my lips as she was if she was sending me kiss.   Geena and I hadn't made love in months.   That night Geena and I made love with a passion that I hadn't seen in years.   The type of love making that makes morning breath insignificant.   I attempted to be delicate, but Geena spoke up.

"Make love to me like you have never before."

A request had been made. I had to step to the plate. I needed to step to the plate. I stepped to the plate. After our early morning love making session, Geena and I feel into a deep comatose like sleep.

I got up the next morning, took a shower, and prepared for work. I boiled an egg and attempted to make a slice of toast and when I heard a stretch and a yawn coming from the bedroom.

"Make me a piece of toast too."

So I threw another slice in the toaster. While I got dressed, I booted my computer to conserve time. When I logged into the internet, my computer immediately spoke to me.

"You've got mail!"

I had one message in my box. I opened the box to see mail from LR _FranklinMD. My first thought was to delete the message, then ignore it, but intrigue had gotten the best of me.   I tiptoed to the bedroom door and peaked in on Geena. She had fallen back into her sleeping comfort zone. I walked back to my computer, opened the email and began to read.

How are you sexy? Haven't heard from you since I got to the city. I hope you're not still mad with me. Just in case you are, I decided to communicate by email. You would love it here. Some of my colleagues took me to the Latin Quarter last Friday. It was so live. I know how much you like salsa and meringue. Speaking of dancing, I'm coming back to Atlanta for Marti

and V's wedding. I was hoping you could be my date. I know
you miss me. I'll call when I get to town. If want to call me,
my cell phone number is (917) 555-7263
   Always,
   Sandy

   Again, I thought about hitting the delete button, but
intrigue got me again. I hit the 'Keep As New' button. Just
then Geena came out of the bedroom. I hadn't heard her get
up.
   "What are you doing? She asked, her words competing
with a yawn that was destined to finish first.
   I jumped when she came out.
   "Nothing."
   I hit the exit button quick. But my computer sold me
out by shouting, "Goodbye!"
   My eyes got big as if to say, "You bitch." By then I was
exposed and about to be investigated.
   "Why were you on the internet this early?"
   "I was checking my emails for work."
   "They just won't let you rest, will they?"
   "Nope. In fact, I need you to drop me off at the plant."
   "Okay...After I eat my toast."
   Geena buttered, jellied, and ate her toast. She threw on
one of the baseball caps I had laying in the closet and we
were out the door. She dropped me off at the gate saying
no one was going to mess with her car. I gave her the
matrimonial kiss before I got out of the car and headed into
the plant.
   As I walked across the floor, I could tell I was the topic
of discussion. I continued as if I didn't notice. I got to the
war room about 8:15, Dave and Rich were talking. It took
me off guard when I saw Dave. He had been working on the
Clorox Project in Forrest Park.
   "What are you doing here? Where's Mike?"
   The room got quiet. I asked the question again.

"Where's Mike?"

Dave looked up from the table.

"That's why I'm here. Mike quit."

"Quit?"

"He called Johnson last night when he got home and resigned."

I was dumbfounded. I knew he was shaken up by what happened the day before, but I didn't think he would quit. I felt awful. I felt like I should have talked to him more. Maybe I should have given him a call when I got home. At that moment, the phone rang. I picked it up and answered, hoping that it would Mike.

"Smith and Boland."

"I thought you were going to be in my office first thing."

It was Towns, I was supposed to meet with him at 8:00. I looked at my watch, it was 8:30.

"We had an impromptu meeting. I'm on my way over now."

I grabbed my notes and headed to the other side of the plant. Before I left, I asked Rich to show Dave Mike's workload. As I walked across the plant, I couldn't help but wonder why Mike didn't call me. Maybe he thought I would try to talk him out of quitting. I would have, but he should have given me the shot. When I got to Towns's office, his assistant ushered me right in.

"Go on in. He's been waiting on you.."

She knew who I was without ever looking up from her computer. I proceeded past her into Towns's office.

"I'm sorry about the delay. We had to expedite some issues this morning."

"Trying to regroup after Old Mike quit, huh?"

"How'd you know Mike quit?"

"Not too much gets past me around here. You see there were a few people around here who saw Mike as one of them. In a few situations he showed them he wasn't."

"Everybody has a job to do Mr. Towns."

"I know that. Do you see me disagreeing with you?"

"So tell me. Who damaged our cars?"

"Don't know that. Not all the information gets to me."

Somehow I felt like Towns knew more than he was letting on. Even though he didn't publicly endorse the behavior. He didn't disrupt it either. I knew I wasn't going to get anywhere from Towns. I changed the subject and went back to the agenda of the meeting.

"I called the meeting to talk to you about hours."

"Okay."

"The way we get close to the dollars we are looking to save, is to reduce hours."

"How pray tell, do you plan to do that?"

"We need to hold layoffs."

"Layoffs? Did you say layoffs?"

"Yes sir."

"How many?"

"30 jobs."

"So you are telling me you want me to layoff 25% of my workforce?"

"Well sir, we need to be in the business of making money."

"We sure are. But let me get this straight. You want me to layoff 30 people just before the holidays? Am I hearing you right?"

When he said that, I felt kinda bad. Then I snapped back to reality. Those fuckers destroyed my car. Fuck them.

"That's what I'm saying."

"Okay...If that's what you want, I think we can do that."

"We?"

"Well you just said...we...we were in the business of making money."

"I'm going to need you in on a couple of meetings. Do you think you can handle that?"

"I'm here to assist you in whatever way I can."

"That's what I want to hear. I'll be calling you."

The meeting went smoother than I thought it would. I couldn't help but think it went a little too smooth. Towns had a little something up his sleeve. But what? I figured I would probably find out sooner than I wanted to.

I got back to the office and checked on Dave to make sure he was catching up with the workload. He was reading some of Mike's reports. Rich had gone to meet with some of his clients.

"How's the reading coming?"

"Mike did some good work. I have a lot of information here."

I mulled over the report folder laying open on my desk.

"Yeah, you do. How long do you think it's going to take you to get caught up?"

"Not long. Give me a couple of days. You're gonna miss a good man."

"I know. Mike was a good guy."

He was not only my co-worker, he was my friend.

23...

spent the next couple of days planning V's bachelor party. I had asked V for some suggestions to feel him out what he wanted to do. I got with Brian, another one of V's groomsmen to trim down the choices. After a small debate we came up with a hotel suite, The Gentleman's Club, and Club Nikki's. We let V choose between the 3. He chose the suite just in case things got as live as we hoped they would. We set the party up for Halloween eve, the weekend prior to his wedding. I stopped by V's house and picked him up. He was dressed to impress. He donned his famous lime-green turtleneck complimented with full cut black trousers. He had buffed his head and over applied the Esi Meoki cologne. He jumped in my rental car excited and ready to roll.

"Where are we going?"

We gave him choices. We made the final selection.

"You'll see brother. Sit back. Kick it and enjoy the ride."

"Ya'll did get the suite?"

"Chill. I got this. Always anxious son."

"I'm ready to get to the women."

I didn't let on, but I was a little excited myself. Neither one of us had been to bachelor party. Neither one of us had ever been in a wedding. His bachelor party was going to be the first and he wanted all rights due a groom taking his last rites. As we got closer to downtown, V was still rattling off hotel names where he thought the party might be.

I pulled in front of the Underground Atlanta Suites Hotel, I valet the car and we got out.

V talked trash like a lion all the way to the hotel. Somehow when we pulled into the driveway, his roar had dropped down to a purr. I could tell he was nervous.

"Don't get nervous now Big Dog."

"I ain't nervous."

"You're nervous."

"I ain't....nervous."

"Well, why did you tip valet twice? You gave him 40 bucks."

"I did?"

He checked his wallet and confirmed what I'd told him.

"Damn. Why didn't you tell me?"

"I thought you were a 'Big Baller-Shot Caller.'"

"Yeah. Okay, smart ass."

I laughed.

We walked into the hotel, the front desk clerk, Duke, gave us the key and we headed up to room 608. When we got to the room, we heard the music going. We slipped in the key and we went on in.

"Wassssuuuuppp!!!!!!!

The crowd shouted. V's face lit up. He saw friends he hadn't in years. There were people there from Pop Warner Football to the Ford Plant. V tried to hold his emotion but his body language told the story. He was happy to see everybody. After the initial hoopla, V walked around and greeted everybody. About 15 minutes in, the topic of discussion changed to the women. Everyone wanted to know where the women were.

Brian halted the party and announced that the entertainment was coming about 11:30, until then we stuck with chips, dip, sea stories, and pornos. The hour and a half before the dancers arrived gave us an opportunity to make declarations of what we do when the dancers did show. Lie or not, the testosterone floating in the room could have killed an ox.

About 11:15 came there was knock at the door. The room got quiet. The tall brother standing by the door opened it. It was security. An Amazon looking sister with a generic burgundy security uniform walked into the room. Her 6 foot, 170 pound physique intimidated every brother in her presence. The only thing humorous about the situation seemed to be her pants, which seemed a size or two too small showing off her huge bottom. The thought on my mind was probably the same as the one on everybody else's, how big was the brother dating this big ass woman?

"Gentlemen, this hotel does not sponsor private parties! I would let it go, but you all are too loud."

She immediately got on the radio.

"Yeah. It's a party. We have about 30 people here. Go ahead and call the police."

The response came back, "10/4."

Duke had taken our tip 2 hours ago, now he was selling us up the river. I wanted to go back down to the desk and get my twenty dollar bill back.

A couple of seconds later...about 10 brothers waiting for the right moment made a mad dash for the door. Explaining your presence at a busted bachelor party wasn't a conversation most brothers were willing to have with their wives. I sat in the corner staring at Brian who was giving me the 'who knew' look.

"Who's in charge here?"

At that moment, there was another knock on the door. The same brother opened it again.

In popped, two fine women who fit the description of dancers. When they saw we were being held hostage by security.

"Oh. I'm sorry. We must have the wrong room." One of the dancers said while they were making a quick exit.

Never really paying attention to the "please help us" expression everyone had. The dancer's mad dash let us know every man for himself...teamwork wasn't the key word for today.

The security went back into her spiel.

"I'll ask again. Who's in charge?"

Everybody pointed at V. He attempted to deny any involvement but nothing would come out.

"I.....I."

"Don't I I now sir, the damage is done. Don't move. The police will be here in a minute."

"But we didn't do nothing. I know we were a little loud but we'll quiet down", V tried plead his case.

"Well, the only way we can get this cleared up....."

"Anything." V responded.

The big Amazon looked V directly in the face.

"You got to get on these!"

She ripped opened her blouse to showing off a full set of perfect breasts. She intentionally placed them in his face. Everybody on the room burst out laughing. The laughter came from an even blend of excitement and relief that security was the show. The Amazon had the body of a goddess. With no clothes on, all of us could see her perfectly sculpted body. She wore her almost 200 pound frame well. The two dancers that had made the quick exit were actually standing in the hallway. They danced their way back into the room. The only person who knew the situation was joke was Brian, who toasted me from across the room.

All the trash talking being sold in the room before the dancers got there had somehow suffered from an illness of broken egos. The talk of ménagetrois and extra curricular sex had given way the approval of exotic dancing and voyeuristic satisfaction.

Later that night when things settled down, it seemed like the right time to pulled out a couple of the Felipe Gregorio cigars that I bought at Martini Club a couple of months ago. I'd been saving them for special occasion, I figured this was a good time to break open the seal.   V, Brian, and I sat on the couch smoking stogeys and sipping VSOP like we were a bunch of bourgeois negroes.   V thanked us for the party and told us how much he appreciated us as friends. There was no thank you needed, he had been there for me when I couldn't call anyone else.

24 . . .

*M*onday morning I went to work late, catching a cab to the Ford dealership on Tara Boulevard. I paid my $500 deductible, picked up my truck and made my way to the plant. I thought about Mike on my way to work and was surprised that he hadn't called me. I figured, I call him up and wake him out of his bed. There wasn't an answer so I left a message for him to call me ASAP. I missed the brother.

Tuesday morning, Mike called. I recognized his phone number coming over my cell.

"What's up, Man? Where have you been?"

"Last couple of days, I've been playing Mr. Mom."

"You like that?"

"Actually it's pretty boring."

"Why'd you quit? ...And why didn't you call me first? I had to hear it from Dave."

"I quit because I had too many close ties to the plant. I couldn't look at those people in the face and talk to them everyday knowing I was going to lay them off in a couple of weeks. I couldn't do it. Besides, it was getting dangerous for my health." Mike laughed. "I didn't call you because you would have talked me into coming back"

"I would have tried."

"That's why I didn't call you."

"So what's your plan?"

"Well I start substitute teaching at the high school next Monday."

I could hear it in his voice...substitute teaching wasn't going to drive his ego for long. He loved consulting.

"Is that going to be fulfilling for you."

"It's a job until something else comes around. Look, I've been spending a lot of time with the girls. More time than I've had in years."

I could tell Mike was trying to justify his new lifestyle.

"Okay, well if you ever want to come back... Call me, bruh."

"I will."

We said our goodbyes and promised to keep in touch.

The rest of the week, I split time between helping V organize his duties for the wedding and trying to get Dave up to speed on the project. He, Rich, and I held several meeting and had business lunches to get up to speed. Dave was a fast learner and didn't need much supervision. He took the ball and ran which was good cause it seemed like V was calling me every 15 minutes.

Wednesday before the wedding I got an opportunity to break away from V to go home and grab a bite.   By the time I got in the house the phone was ringing. I answered the phone pretty abruptly, I'd told V, I would be right back.

"Damn! Can I get something to eat? I said I would be right back."

"I'm sorry sexy. I didn't know you were eating."

It was Sandy. She was back in Atlanta. I kept hoping something would come up and she wouldn't be able to make it back.

"Where are you?"

"What do mean? Where am I?

"As in Atlanta or New York?"

"Where did I say I was going to be?"

"Ahhh...In Atlanta?"

"Correctamundo? Are you coming to see me?"

"Where's your man?"

"I don't have a man."

"Sandy. Let's not go through this again."

"Whatever."

"Where are you?" I asked.

"I'm staying at a friend's house in Vinings."

"Who lives in Vinings?"

"A friend."

"I'm going to leave it alone. I got to meet V at the reception hall. I'll call you back. What's the number?"

"Just call me on my cell."

"You can't give me the number?"

"I don't know the number. Call me on my cell."

A couple of months ago, Sandy accused me of not being truthful. I suddenly realized both of us had lived double lives. At that moment, I started asking myself, "Who am I?"

I didn't recognize myself. Once again my life was spinning beyond control. I could see it. I could feel it. But I couldn't control it. She was like a drug.

I ran back to the reception hall and showed my face, but my mind was elsewhere and I knew it. I was wondering why she even came back. She was 700 miles away. She wasn't that close to V or Marti. Why? I couldn't tell Geena, she wasn't invited. I was caught up AGAIN. Damn! But I had to see Sandy. I had to look in her face. I called her and got the directions to her friend's house. I took me 30 minutes, I finally arrived at the Vinings Townhouses. It was huge complex running in 500G range complete with guard at the gate. The guard called the house and Sandy ok'd me in. I was still wondering who was the friend. I quickly found out when one of the neighbors asked me if Trotter was home. I decided not to tell Sandy that I knew it was Kevin's house to see if she would tell me. As I approached the door, I began to get nervous. My heart was pounding so hard it could have jumped through my chest and knocked on the door itself. I rang the doorbell and waited. Sandy opened the door wearing a full body linen dashiki, the silhouette of her body melted through the fabric as the light hit it. Wearing no bra, her breasts penetrated the material as if they were needles poking into a piece of fabric. I got the feeling she intentionally wore black thong panties because she knew my attention would have been instantly drawn to her ass. She gave me a sensuous kiss on the lips as soon as I walked through the door.

"How are you?" She asked.

"I'm good. You look good. Long time no see."

"So do you."

"How do you like this dashiki? I got it in the Village."

"It looks good. Whose house is this?"

"A friend's."

"What friend?"

At that moment, Sandy got up from the living room chair she was sitting in and walked towards me. On her way, she spoke in defense of her statement.

"My friend. Nobody important."

She grabbed my face and began kissing me.

"Tell me you missed me."

She kissed me again and slid over and nibbled my ear lobe.

"Tell me you missed this."

She kissed me again grabbing my hands placing them on her hips. I gave in for a second.

"Tell me." She said again.

For the first time in my life, I saw how selfish Sandy was. It was all about her. I pulled away.

"What? What's wrong?" Sandy asked.

I suddenly lost it.

"Why are you such a liar?!" I spoke louder than normal, not quite yelling.

"What are you talking about?"

"Whose house is this?"

"A friend's. Why are you trippin'?"

"You are the trip. You were going to fuck me in Kevin's house?"

"Who says this is Kevin's house?"

"The neighbors, Sandy!"

She was dumbfounded, but she didn't take any ownership in her behavior. As far as Sandy was concerned 'game was suppose to recognize game.'

"You know. I didn't realize how selfish you really are until now. You've never told me you love me. You've never said you missed me. You've always asked if I missed you. It's always been about you. Hasn't it?"

"What are you talking about?" She tried to defend herself.

"Cut the shit, Sandy. You know. Look at you. You opened the door practically butt-naked. Even when you sent the email, you said, DO YOU MISS ME? I KNOW YOU DO."

She just sat there. I didn't know if she was gathering her thoughts or if I'd left her speechless. At that point, I didn't care. I kept going.

"Today, I suddenly realized something. I've been fighting for your love for three years. I just realized the person who I've been fighting was you. You! I've been fighting for you...with you. When I got too close, you'd step away. But only enough, so I could chase you again. How perverted was that? I was the only person who ever knew there was competition. None of the other brothers you dated knew. You've had me jumping through hoops against nobody. ...And you watched me do it. Fuck this. I'm out."

Sandy just sat there looking at me. She watched me head for the door, then it sunk in. I had just cursed her ass out. By the time I hit the crack of the door, she was livid. I heard her run to the door.

"Fuck You! You hear me! Fuck You!"

I never looked back. I smiled as I cranked up the Expedition. At that moment, I felt free. But free of what? I didn't know, but there was a lot of free therapy that just happened.

I stopped at the Stop 'n Go, bought me a Snickers, and passed my player's jersey to the little kid on the Huffy riding by. In my mind, I wished him better luck than I'd had.

25 . . .

riday came quick. I had been running with V all week. Ruffled about Sandy being in town and the thought of her and Geena both coming to the wedding was aging me faster than a butterfly in the summer time. I kept my priorities in perspective and stayed focused on the job. I was finishing up a meeting with Dave and Rich when Towns called.

"What are you doing, College Boy?"

I laughed. I was used to Towns. He brought the comic relief to a tough job.

"I'm finishing up a meeting, Mr. Towns."

"Call me back when you get a chance."

"No. We can talk now. I've got time."

I broke off the last of our meeting to concentrate on Towns.

"I got some things going before lunch. I need your input. When do you think you can come down to my office?"

"I have some things to finish up. How does 11:00 sound?"

"Good. I'll expect you then."

I got off the phone feeling that Towns and I were finally beginning to work as a team. I'd begun to get excited by the possibility of he and I making the project successful. He was asking for my input and teamwork. I finished my reports in just enough time to get to Towns' office by eleven. When I got there, Towns was sitting in a meeting with two more people. The Union Chairman and HR rep.

"Do I need to come back?"

"No. This meeting is for everybody. I need you here."

When I came in, Towns introduced me. But Towns knew he had me wondering why I needed to be in a meeting with HR and the Union. I stayed quiet in hopes of gaining more information. Before I could say another word, one of the assemblymen came into the room. I could tell by the assemblyman's behavior, he was a stranger to what was going on as well. Towns went into a little spiel about how valuable the worker was to the company, but due to a loss in profits, he was going to have to let him go.

"Felix, we'd really like to keep you, but due to the fact that the consulting firm has recommended a layoff, we're gonna follow their lead."

Towns had strategically put me in the crosshairs of every union employee in the plant and he knew it. I sat quietly, feeling helpless and responsible at the same time Felix was begging for his job. Offering to take a pay cut, move to another job, not take his bonus, anything not to lose his job. He asked the panel for answers, solutions to how he was supposed to fund his family's Christmas. No one spoke up. They kept to business at hand. Firing folks and escorting them to the gate. After Felix left, I attempted to make a dash for the door.

"Where you goin' College Boy?"

"I don't need to be here."

"Yes you do. We've got 29 more of these to go. You've been talking about choices and decisions since you've been here. These are hard choices and decisions that have to be made. The choices where a consulting team makes recommendations and tries to exclude themselves from the consequences. Well this is the consequence, College Boy, and I want you here."

"I'm leaving." I stood strong.

Towns fired back, "You aren't goin' nowhere. I got permission from your boss, Tom Johnson. He wants you here too." Towns winked at me. He had set me up. Done his homework. Or did he?

"I need to call my boss." I said to Towns trying to feel him out. He handed me the phone. I declined and stepped into a side office and called Johnson. I laid my platform out to Johnson. Telling him that this was unprecedented and me being in the room added no value to the situation.

His response, "They are paying us $40,000 a week. If they want you in there, I want you there. I hung up. Seeing there was no way out barring losing my job. Bastard, sold me out for $40,000. I shuffled back to the room as if I were in a Amos 'n Andy episode and slimed back into my chair thinking, 'I's a do anythangs you tells me. I needs this good job.'

One after another, I sat there watching each worker being let go. Some went humbly, others went fighting. Security had to remove them. Every situation printed a stamp on my psyche. Towns was showing me his shoes and not only did he show them to me; he was asking me to try them on. I didn't like the way they felt. The next person called was Vladimir Williams. V walked in. Sat down. Towns went into his spiel. I never looked up from the table. Looking at cedar presented a better view than having to look V directly in the face. My boy since the 5th grade, the best man at his wedding and I selling him out. V sat there staring at me. He didn't look at Towns. He didn't look at his union rep. He didn't look at Human Resources. He sat there focused on me. I could feel his eyes burning through my flesh. V sat there quietly like a slave refusing to have his dignity squandered. Refusing to show any weaknesses. After it was over, V stood up, removed his union pin in protest, placed it on the table, and walked from the room.

After all was said and done, I felt no better. I felt like I had snatched bread from the very people who'd allowed me to have a job in the first place. I excused myself. Before I could get to my office my cell phone rang.

"Hello."

"This is V."

"Look bruh. I'm sorry about..."

"Hey. I don't want to talk now. But I was just calling to ask you not to come to rehearsal or the dinner."

"If that's what you want. Can I ask question? Am I..."

V was gone by the time I got to 'want'. He never heard the rest of the question.

"In the wedding?"

Suddenly what just happened had gotten under my skin. I wasn't liking me very much now. In fact, not at all. Before I could think, I was calling Johnson. His voicemail picked up.

"Mr. Johnson. I resign."

I packed my computer bag and left without saying goodbye to Rich or Dave.

I left the plant needing to be alone. I needed to clear my mind. I decided to take a drive. I got on I-75 heading downtown. Did I quit too soon? I asked Mike earlier in the week if he thought he was quitting too soon and here I was doing the same thing. There were emotional demands that went along with the job. Towns had been trying to teach me a lesson in wisdom the whole time and I was too arrogant to learn the lesson. There is always a chapter in redemption that is yet to be written. I was living out the book. My mind was racing. Had it cost me a friendship? I was sure V would understand when he found out I resigned. The look in his eyes told me we needed to talk. Soon. I got off the expressway just short of downtown, exiting at Turner Field, I turned left on Abernathy Drive. I still didn't know where I was going. I was headed in the direction of several places. My parent's house, The AU Center, Geena's. Whenever I've had issues, I'd drive down to AU. Seeing the students going to class reminded me of when I was there. They traveled the campus enjoying life. What frat or sorority was having the weekend party? Who had the notes from Professor So-and-So's Class? Except for the tuition payment that was due before finals, life was always good. We all had our own ideologies about how we were going to change the world. But, how many of us would actually stand up for change after graduation? Or would we give in to the comforts of the corporate lifestyle? Clark had taught us the theory. They taught it well. But they never taught us there were certain alliances that had to be relied upon to survive in the world of office politics. I had to learn that on my own. Before I knew it, I was in the heart of the Atlanta University Center. The hard rain and cold had sent the students scrambling for cover inside the lecture halls throughout the campus. After a few turns, I was at Martin Luther King Drive. Looking at the city skyline to my right, I turned left deciding to steer clear of rush hour traffic.

As I drove down Martin Luther King, I stared at the thugs, hustlers, and vagrants seemingly conducting street business along the street. I wondered why I saw the illegal transactions going down with little or no interaction from my friends in blue. It made me wonder if the same types of businesses would have been endorsed in Buckhead. I answered the question without even having to uttered a word. Here was a street named after the father of the non-violent civil rights movement. It didn't matter what major city you went to, hanging out on King for any extended period of time could cost you your life. Why? As I began to question my theories about life, I knew I was beginning to come back to earth. Acting more like myself. Before I knew it I was in Adamsville, a section of town not far from Geena's house.

By this time I was ready to talk. I took the left on Fairburn and headed to Geena's. Five minutes later, I was at her house. She wasn't home. I decided to go inside and wait. The house was dark, the light of day was quickly fading behind the blinds to the back yard. I looked in the refrigerator, grabbed a bowl of Geena's famous stuffing she had left over from the previous day. After nuking it, I sat on her sofa, cut the TV on and relaxed a little. I flipped through the channels until I settled on Oprah. It was one of her Dr. Phil episodes. The topic of the day was trust. "Geez. Why today?" My therapy continued. I sat there and watched people talk about trust with total strangers when I had trust issues with people I dealt with everyday. During one of the commercials, my eyes caught a glimpse of a small purple book propped under the In Style and Essence magazines sitting on the coffee table. I was unmistakably drawn to the energy of the book. I didn't know if I chose the book or the book chose me. I picked it up. When I opened it. Poetry was everywhere. They were all dated. Geena had been expressing herself in poems and prose for the last 10 years. I read one poem after another. I was blown away at the talent and energy that poured from her feelings. Instead of an autobiography, she had told her life story through the cloak of poetry. The poems were intense, funny, painful, and honest. Titles like Project Life, One Man Woman, and Generations told me different stories about Geena that I matched to certain periods in her life. I turned to page 147, when I stopped to read a poem that she had written during one of the periods when we were broken up.

August 27, 19__
I Remember...
I remember as though it were yesterday...
The confidence in his stride as he made his way gallantly toward
me.
The world was his and he knew it.
He came, like a thief in the night,
Unexpected and swift...but I welcomed him into my world ...

As though I had been awaiting his arrival all of my life.
I remember his eyes…dark, deep and full of life,
With lashes so long
They reached out and tickled my ear as he gently kissed my neck.
His eyes penetrated my soul with kindness and sincerity
Like I'd never experienced before and I knew…
He was the "The One."
I remember his smile…
A sheepish grin and a boyish charm,
Keeping a secret that we all wished we knew.
I remember his fervor and passion for life…
Never the spectator…always the participant.
He draws the distant near with his wit, charm and humor.
I wonder if he knows the spell he casts on those within his midst?
I remember the way he loved me…
Slowly, methodically…kissing, caressing and penetrating every inch
that was me.
He loved me in a way that only he could, reaching the core of my
femininity.
But most of all I remember he left…just as quickly as he came.
Like a thief in the night, he gathered what he came for and never
looked back.

She had predicted I would leave her several years ago. At
that moment, I looked to my right. Staring me in the face
was a picture Geena and I had taken together at a wedding
of one her friends from Tech School. I studied both of our
features, I looked as though I was going through the
motions. Her expression was worth a pot of gold. The
photo spoke a thousand words. She was where she wanted to
be. Where she was suppose to be. My emotions were
suddenly bouncing off the walls. I was in the process of
taking inventory when I heard a key entering the front door
lock. I quickly put the book back in it's place and pretended
that my attention was being fully occupied by Oprah and
Dr. Phil. Geena bum rushed the room weighted down with

shopping bags in both hands.

"What are you doing here?"   She said gathering her breath.

"Just left work. Decided to come over."

"You are using that key a little more these days."

"Be quiet."

"You shut up. I want you to look at something."

Before I could get a word out, she had grabbed her bags and ran back to her bedroom.

Me, Oprah, and Dr. Phil could hear bags ripping and packages tearing. Five minutes later, Geena reappeared in a semi-formal black maternity cocktail dress and big cheesy smile.

"How do I look?"

She stood there looking at me waiting on an answer, visibly pregnant and glowing.

"You look good."

"Just good.?"

"You look beautiful...." She heard my hesitation.

"What's wrong with you?"

"I quit my job."

"You quit your who?"

"I quit my job."

"Why?"

"V got laid off. I recommended the layoff."

"You did what?! He's getting married tomorrow."

"I know that!"

"What'd he say?"

"He didn't say anything. He didn't say a word. He stared at me and walked out of the room."

"Have you talked to him since?"

"He left me a message saying don't come to the rehearsal or dinner. He needed to focus on what was happening."

This time Geena was consoling me. Sitting next to me. Her hand on my shoulder. She stood up and hugged me. I laid my head on her stomach and attempted to make light of everything that was happening. I returned the first hard embrace I'd given her in years. She returned it, feeling my need to be held. Just as I began to break away a tiny push lifted my head off her stomach. I looked up at Geena. Her eyes were saying the same thing I was thinking.

"Did you feel that?" She screamed laughing.

"I did. What was that?"

"The baby kicked!"

"The baby kicked?!"

"Yes."

"I felt it."

We stood there embracing each other and laughing. What I thought would be a moment of despair turned out to be the most satisfying moment of my life. Geena and I were celebrating the evolution of a new life and for the first time I actually felt like this was where I was suppose to be. It was bitter-sweet though. I felt like I gaining a family and losing a friend.

26 . . .

I got to the church about noon. As I walked through, nobody spoke. It was Marti's day but I got the feeling I was the spotlight. One of the ushers pointed me in the direction of the groom's dressing room. I followed the directions to the bottom floor of the church. I could hear a small amount of laughter, but the atmosphere was somber. I started to knock but disregarded that thought and walked in. When I hit the door the conversations stopped. V was getting dressed behind a partition and talking over it.

"I tell you, I was just sitting there. I couldn't believe it. ...And you know what, I didn't say nothing. I just looked at him. He couldn't even look me in the face. But you never know who your friends are. What's up with yall? Why are you guys so quiet? ...Brian?"

There was no response. The room was quiet. As my eyes scanned the room, I began to take inventory of who was present. Mr. Williams, V's father. Mr. Murray, Marti's father. Brian and the rest of the groomsmen. As I panned the room, my shoes dropped from my hand and hit the floor. V was still asking questions.

"What was that? Don't break nothing. 'Cause I can't afford to come back from a honeymoon paying for stuff."

Still no response. I decided to speak up.

"My fault."

V recognized my voice immediately. He looked from behind the partition.

"What's up man? How long have you been here?"

"A minute or two. I thought you were going to pick me up on the way to the church?"

"I overslept and had to get to the church quick this morning. My fault."

"Is there anything you want to tell me V."

"What?"

"Is there anything you want to tell me?"

After a bit of hesitation. V answered.

"Ahhh. Yeah I do. Let's step outside in the hallway."

I followed V out of the room like I was in trouble and following my teacher to the principal's office. V had gotten fully dressed in his tux and I wore the sweats that I'd rushed to put on 30 minutes before I hit the steps of the church. As V started to talk, I sensed the hesitation in his voice.

"I was thinking. Ummm. I was thinking...I don't think it's going to be good idea for you to be my best man."

"Why?"

"Do you have to ask me why? I'll tell you what. I'll give you three guesses and when you get hot, I'll let you know."

"Yesterday."

"Batta Boom Batta Bang."

"Look I didn't know that was going down like... It was Towns that..."

"But you endorsed it. You did. I know it. I never would have thought my boy would have sold me out. Not only that. The day before my wedding."

"Man. I didn't know."

I was standing begging V for another chance like a boyfriend begging his lover after he'd fucked up.

"Man, it wasn't my fault." I pleaded.

"I tell you what...I don't want you there. But I know I asked you to be my best man and if you want to do it, it's your call."

I wanted to say yeah. I wanted to say I understood. But the situation was cloudy. It was downright fucked up. I looked at V. His look told me what I already knew. I could feel that I had betrayed him more than I would ever know. V had posed me with a question that I'd never thought he'd ever have to ask. He was questioning our friendship. My loyalty.

"Go ahead. Do your thing. I'm getting dressed."

V walked away. A few minutes later, the groom and the groomsmen were headed to the sanctuary. As I got dressed, I could hear noises behind the door. As I peeked out, I saw Marti and her bridesmaids. She looked beautiful. ...As if she were always meant to be a bride. Her bridesmaids made up all the colors of the rainbow. Each wore different pastel colors...Mint, Lemon, Powder Blue, Soft Pink, and Lavender. While I finished getting dressed a thousand scenarios ran through my head. Was I right or was I being selfish? I tried to convince myself I was the best man. I was the one asked. I finished tying my tie walking out the door. By the time I got to the vestibule, Marti was already lined up in the wedding processional. We made eye contact. She motioned her lips.

"Hi."

I motioned back, "You're beautiful."

"Thank you."

It was Marti's day. Not my time to make a stand. I stood at the corner and watched as each bridesmaid's turn came up to walk down the aisle. Before Marti left, she looked my way motioning her lips.

"Bye. I love you."

"I love you too."

Like that she was gone.

I walked into the sanctuary and sat next to Geena. She looked at me with a solace and comfort on her face to let me know she understood and she was there for me. She clinched my hand and held it during the ceremony. Geena was always and forever my supporter. I watched as Brian stood in my place and handed V the ring. Tears, laughter, joy, and sadness filled the room. But the sadness only came from me.

Geena and I left the church, dropped off our wedding gift and went home. I was suddenly stared in the face by the fact that I had a pregnant girlfriend, no best friend, and no job. What was next...

I didn't see V after that day. When I would see our friends, I'd ask about him and Marti. One Sunday after church, Geena and I ran into Brian at the Shark Bar Brunch. He told me Marti had given birth to baby girl they named Mina. He was going to school to get a Microsoft certification. But they were fine. That was good. Cause I prayed that they would be.

27

I awoke in the middle of the night to Geena standing over me.

"Wake up. Wake Up. It's time."

Still groggy, "Time for what?"

"The baby's coming. Wake up."

At first I thought I was dreaming but then my conscious brain kicked in.

"Oh shit. The baby's coming! Baby, get up the baby's coming!"

Geena had already gotten up and taken a shower and gotten dressed. I threw on some warm-ups, grabbed Geena's suitcase and headed to the hospital. Geena and I had switched roles. She was the calm one and I nervous as hell. I tried to call my parents on my cell phone but nervously dropped it in my lap.

Geena shouted, "Don't kill me!" As I swerved back onto my side of the road. "Keep your eyes on the road! I'll do it!" Geena managed to get the phone and call our parents to meet us at the hospital.

By the time we got to the hospital, the baby was coming. The nurses immediately rushed Geena to the delivery room. I was following right behind when one of the nurses stopped me and said she'd let me know when I could come in. Just as I settled into the visitor's room, Geena's mother walked

walked through the door.

"What's happening? How is she?"

"She's good. I guess they're getting her ready. They said they'd be back to get me."

"Well they need to hurry up so I can get some information."

I laughed thinking she was older version of Geena.

"It's cool. We'll be able to see her in a minute."

At that moment, my parents rushed through the door asking the same questions Geena's mother had just asked. Geena's mother stepped to the plate and filled them in even though she had just gotten second hand information from me. Ten minutes later, the nurse came back to the visitor's room.

"ReGeena Douglass' party?"

Geena's mother jumped up.

"That's me." She staked claim to her middle born child.

I added my little bit. "That's me too."

"Oh yeah. He's the daddy."

"...And the husband." I added.

The nurse smiled at our rivaling behavior, "Well the two of you come with me."

I hugged my mother and D then Geena's mother and I headed into the unknown.

Things had happened so fast in the last 6 months. Geena and I had decided, planned and pulled off a wedding ceremony in Gatlinburg, Tennessee. It was a nice ceremony. Looking over the Appalachian hilltops. My father was my best man. During the ceremony, I'd wished V and Marti could have been there. We hadn't spoken in months. But I had gotten used to life without talking to my best friend. A couple of times, I'd thought about going to the Run 'n Shoot, but backed out at the last minute. I moved in with Geena when we got back from Gatlinburg. It was definitely an adjustment. But I did have something new. Geena cooked everyday. A home cooked meal everyday was something I hadn't had since I lived with my mother and father.

While Geena's mother and I were getting gowned, the nurse briefed us on what to expect. Our do's and don't. Before I went in the nurse gave me a small pep talk.

"Remember, you're the coach. She's the player. Her confidence depends on you."

She made me a little nervous. I tried not to show it, but I think she sensed it. I thought back 7 _ months ago, this moment almost didn't happen. But it was happening and I was ready. Geena and I had decided to be surprised by the sex of the baby, so the doctor never let us know. Geena refused the epidural shot saying the first time she wanted to feel the path of motherhood being exhumed from her body.

By the time we got to the delivery room, Geena was screaming. When I came around the corner, I thought to myself where have I heard that scream before. Geena attacked me as soon as I hit the door.

"It was you! That's the bastard!"

I looked around to see who she was talking to. Geena's mother looked at me and assisted with the abuse.

"Bastard." As she rushed over to Geena. "Mommy's here with you baby."

"Baby. You look so beautiful." I put my hand on her forehead.

"Keep your fucking hands off of me! Don't you ever touch me again!"

I couldn't believe I was getting abused like this.

The nurse came walked over and whispered.

"Don't worry. They act like this during transition."

Over the next two hours, I watched Geena scream, holler, and curse everyone in the room. About halfway through, I almost ran out and called an exorcist. My mind might have been playing tricks on me but I could have sworn I saw Geena's head spin around once or twice. I pulled out the surprise camcorder to record this sacred event, but my plan was quickly thwarted.

"If you don't cut that shit off, I'll cut off your balls!"

I cut it off and followed the orders of Lorena Bobbitt formerly known as the Exorcist.

Finally relief came when the doctor said the magic words.

"I see a head!"

Geena laid back and took a deep breath and so did I. He followed that up with another command.

"We aren't done. Keep pushing. That's just the head."

The screaming started again. Ten minutes later, the baby's shoulders followed a smooth transition through the rest of the process. Geena laid back again. Out of breath she asked, "What is it?" The doctor yelled. "You have a beautiful baby boy." Geena smiled.

At the first moment, the baby didn't cry. But after a slap on the bottom, he let out a loud roar.

Geena's mother laughed out, "Yeah that's Geena's baby."

Geena tried to gather her composure, but the tears flowed like a river. Geena and I had come full circle and it was wonderful feeling minus a few curse words in the last few hours. But everything else was all good. When I held my son the first time, I looked at him; my eyes watered up. I looked to the sky and asked God.

"Please protect my son."

I wanted to hold him to the heavens the way Kunta held up Kizzy, but decided I'd wait until we got home.

When he left the hospital his name would be Christian Ahmad Douglass.

When I left Smith and Boland, I picked up several jobs consulting as a contract analyst. A few months later, Dave called and gave me tip that a hospital needed an analysis. The firm wasn't going to take it. It was too small for them. I made a few phone calls and got the job. I kissed Geena and Christian bye for a couple of days and got on a plane.

Five days later, I was going over my analysis with the

hospital staff. When I finished I was bombarded with question after question. I answered most. Referred a few to the chief of staff. After about 45 minutes, I asked if there was one last question. A white coat poked from the crowd.

"How is this change going to effect our manpower. We're already short handed."

It was Sandy. She'd been there the whole time. Her curly natural was now long and straight. Her Rae Dong look had been replaced by that of a mature professional woman. I answered her question, which she seemed pleased to get. For a moment we were transported somewhere else mentally but I came back. When I finished my answer. The chief of staff stepped in.

"Thank you for the question, Doctor Trotter."

She tilted her head in acknowledgement. Dr. Trotter. She had married Kevin. She looked happy. After the meeting, we talked for a brief moment.

"Congratulations Dr. Trotter. When was the marriage?"

"A couple of months ago. We did it in Jamaica."

She looked at my left ring finger and spotted a platinum band on mine.

"Is that ring telling me something? Should I be congratulating you also?"

"Yeah. Geena and I followed your advice."

"That's good." She said. Then whispered, "I really didn't mean it."

I laughed. She copied with her patented signature giggle. The one that only identified her. I looked in her green eyes searching for something. A spot search for an answer to why this woman once had such a powerful effect on me. Even though she was still beautiful, the magnetism was gone. I suddenly felt a vibration on my hip. My pager was going off. I looked down, it was Geena.

We luv U. Can't wait 4 U to get home.
PS...your boy is bad (smile)

I looked back up at Sandy. There was nothing to search for. By early evening I was on a plane headed back to the ATL. Heading back to my family.

I got home about 8 o'clock that evening. I could hear Christian mad crawling to meet me at the door followed by his mother. They met me with a kiss and a hug.

"How was your trip? Did you meet anyone interesting?" There was that woman's intuition thing kicking in again.

"Naw. It was just a job. Couldn't wait to get home." I gave her a hard passionate kiss.

"Whew. I need to send you on the road more often." We laughed.

About a month later, we were watching TV. An episode of Will and Grace about honesty.

"Can I ask you something?"

"What?"

"How did you know about Sandy?"

She smiled.

"Honestly?"

"Honestly." I concurred.

"You checked your messages from my phone and you left the code in the display. I had your voice mail code."

I should have been upset but then I thought to myself, "Don't hate the player. Hate the game."

28 ...

got to the office for some meetings early this morning. My father was already here. Grunting out commands like he was in charge. This was his baby. When I got a little time, I pulled him aside and told him not to be so hard on folks. He smiled and said he just wanted everything to look good. I understood. By the end of the day, my mother, Geena and Christian had rolled through. I had to pop him on the butt twice for continuing to pull my papers off my desk. He just looked at me and smiled. I'd catch him in trouble and call his name. He'd look over at me with honest eyes.

"I wuv yu dada."

Before I could get mad. My heart had already melted. I watched his mannerisms and his movements.

"That's my boy."

Geena spent about 3 hours at the office, typing memos and doing anything she could to help. Then she and Christian headed home. I told her I'd be right behind them. After studying report after report and document and after document, it was 4 hours later and my eyes were starting to slam shut. I was gathering my things to leave when I heard a noise in the front room.

"Who's there? I'm only going to say it once."

There was no answer.

"Who's there?" I said it again.

I grabbed my baseball bat from the corner thinking it better be somebody with some rib tips. Before I could break the plane of the door, A voice said, "Whoa. Don't hurt'em Hammer."

It was V.

"Well you know how I used to do it in high school."

"You rode the bench in high school."

"I had a breakout game against Therrell in '84."

Both of us tried to hold it, but burst out laughing.

"What's been happening, man?"

"Not too much. Family life."

"I feel ya. Me too."

"I thought the next city councilman might need some help on his campaign. Looks like you need some of my expertise around here."

"I do. Anything you can do bruh, I would appreciate."

"I want to be a part of something special."

"Having you on the team is special enough.   About what happened…"

"Don't worry about it. It's in the past."

V gave me a hug. We held our composure. But it was an undeniable fact that two grown ass men had water in their eyes. We spent the next two hours getting caught up and joking as if we'd never stopped. My boy was back.

Acknowledgements

First of all, I want to give thanks to where it truly belongs, with God Almighty. Without you, none of this would have been possible. Secondly, I got to thank my editor Angie Jackson, who gave me the best chance to see this complete. You were as cool as the other side of the pillow. I know it was a task dealing with me.

My mother, Norma Cleveland-Parham, what can I say? You've been my savior, my protector, and my friend. There is no amount of thanx that will equal what I owe you. I say thank- you to God each day for your existence. But I would also like to thank you for giving me that piece of advice when I said I wanted to be a writer. "If you want to write, then write, but never stop reading. That's what's important." I won't. And you know she wasn't going to let me mention her without giving a shout out to everybody at Guaranty. You all have been so nice to me. Christine Pickens and Carolyn Hightower, the Super Bowl and card parties reminded me of you. Unlimited Elegance in the house. Can't forget my father, David Cleveland...Thank you for all the life experiences you gave me. They made me stronger.

Vonnie, my angel, you have always looked out and this time was no exception. I could have sworn I saw wings hidden under your shirt. Don't fly away. Ms. Smith and Mr. and Mrs. Martin, you know I couldn't leave you out. Look a there, you made the book. My Aunt Phyllis, thanks for reading my first semblance of a manuscript in confidence and letting me believe I had some talent and my Uncle Jerry who would correct me each time I said "if" my book gets published and replaced it with "when." My grandfather, Toby Belle, you've always been "THE MAN." In times of trouble, your advice came in handy (smile). Tricky (Toni Richardson)!!! Thanx for the love with the poetry. Couldn't have done this thing without you. Your book is next. Sheryl Jones M.D. of Memphis, Tennessee, thanx for having so many books for me to read. I told you

I had a book in me. ....And Kelvaleski Davis, you are the man on the real. To you, a million thank-you's. All of them counting back to the 5th grade. A special thanx to Mrs. Renia Davis, I still love you even if you were stingy with the buddy passes. I also want to give a shout out to Ty who kept us laughing back in the day. You are a straight fool. You'd hold your own in "joning" session any day.

Sweet Potato Pye, you have given me so much love. Thank-you for your patience. I love you. Alexandra, my little baby or should I say my big girl. Keep up the good work. Daddy really is... proud of you. Tuna, I don't have to say it but I will, again...you really are a great mom. I hope you are here forever. Forever, ever. Papa, Granny...I could never leave you out of this equation, BAM!

Sarah Miller, thanx for the cover...from the first time I saw your work, I knew you would be a great artist. I just wanted to be one of the first on the Sarah Miller bandwagon...I got my trumpet, girl. Doctor K, my partner in crime, thank you for the inspiration and not to mention a little leadership. We are going to the top with this thing. My Alabama peeps, Gwen, Koriya, Koriael, and Pretty Tony, thanx for the love. I didn't leave you out, Rod. Buy my book. I bought your t-shirt.

Carol Addyman and her staff @ Addyman Design, what can I say, the best graphic artists in the world. ...and reasonable too. You know I'm laughing. Olaf Guerrero, my man representing the country of Belize. Thank you for the website, You did an outstanding job. Lori P. and Mrs. Hitt in Newport News, thanx for answering my questions when I had them. Lori, stop smiling. Albert K. and Laurie D. thank-you for the marketing stuff, I needed it. Ray Culpepper, thanx for hitting me in the head. It took a minute, but I finally realized that I needed to get my own thing. Tara B. in Dallas thank-you for lending an ear when I needed someone to talk to. To my Clark Atlanta crew in LA and Atlanta, thanx for keeping me grounded, I can get beside myself sometimes. Mays High...that seems so long ago...but those times were the best. I wish I had known it then. Candy...you always are in charge and Kim Shivers, it's the sixth to the last sentence, but you made it. Did I forget anyone? Oh yeah! Cherrio...you are what I miss most about LA. If I left anyone out, hit me on the email (Nigel_Reynard@hotmail.com). I'll put you first in the next one.

About the Author

Nigel Reynard was born in Birmingham, Alabama and raised on the Southwest side of Atlanta, Georgia. The former consultant and first time writer received his Bachelor's Degree from Clark Atlanta University in Radio, Television, and Film. He lived in Los Angeles for 4 years and returned home to Atlanta to work on his first novel entitled "In Due Time". He is currently working on his second book, not yet titled.